This job was everything she a ever wanted.

She'd practically broken her back to become the top chef at one of Manhattan's best restaurants, and she wasn't about to blow it all in one emotional outburst.

Assembling each dish methodically, her thoughts returned to Tom. He was virtually the only man alive who knew the weak and needy Jessica. It was far too dangerous to be thinking of Tom in terms of whirly-twirlies. That would never do. She could show her best friend that side of her, but never the man she intended to marry. Her father was right—it was fine to want a man, but not to need one.

And she needed Tom.

KRISTIN BILLERBECK lives in California's beautiful Gold Country with her husband and four small children. Besides writing, Kristin loves reading, outings with her family, and eating out! Visit her on the Web at www.kristinbillerbeck.com or e-mail her at KrisBeck@aol.com.

NANCY TOBACK has been married to her evangelist husband Jack for eighteen years. She has two adult children and a twelve-year-old son. Nancy was born and raised in Manhattan and now resides in Long Beach, New York, about forty minutes from the Big Apple. When there's spare time after being wife, mother, and writer, Nancy enjoys being watercolorist, charcoal artist, and cooking gourmet food.

Books by Kristin Billerbeck

HEARTSONG PRESENTS
HP247—Strong as the Redwood
HP294—To Truly See
HP329—Meet My Sister, Tess
HP378—The Landlord Takes a Bride
HP448—The Prodigal Welcome
HP454—Grace in Action
HP565—An Unbreakable Hope

Don't miss out on any of our super romances. Write to us at the following address for information on our newest releases and club information.

Heartsong Presents Readers' Service
PO Box 721
Uhrichsville, OH 44683

Love Online

Kristin Billerbeck and Nancy Toback

Heartsong Presents

In loving memory of my dear, sweet sister Annette—my best friend.
Thank you for your encouragement and prayers.
I'll so miss your smile, though I know you are in a far better
place now, in the arms of our heavenly Father.
I love you.
Nancy

A note from the Authors:

We love to hear from our readers! You may correspond with
us by writing:

Kristin Billerbeck and Nancy Toback
Author Relations
PO Box 719
Uhrichsville, OH 44683

ISBN 1-58660-927-0

LOVE ONLINE

All Scripture quotations are taken from the King James Version of the
Bible.

Our mission is to publish and distribute inspirational products offering
exceptional value and biblical encouragement to the masses.

PRINTED IN THE U.S.A.

one

Tom lowered the truck's electric window and squinted at the hazy gray sky. A smidgen of sunshine broke through the clouds. He should've gone to the Bronx Zoo with Frank—and the promise of "the blind date from heaven."

At the blare of a car horn, Tom punched the accelerator, drove through the intersection, and turned right. He glided to a stop in the tow-away zone in front of Jessica's apartment building.

Instead of a romantic possibility at the zoo, he'd opted to eat up his Saturday morning in a bridal shop. He knew the routine. This would be Jessica's sixth march down the aisle as a bridesmaid. He'd been there for the previous five fittings—driven to distraction as Jess stood poised on a platform, a seamstress pinning material around the perfect curves of her tall, slender frame.

Tom scrubbed his hand across his jaw and huffed out a deep breath. After sixteen years as her friend, he knew she'd never see him as anything more. Yet here he was, as faithful as ever, by her side. He had to be kidding himself. He shot a glance at her building. The spike of self-pity in his gut disintegrated at the sight of Jess, whirling past the doorman, a smile lighting her gorgeous features.

The concierge pulled open the truck door. "Thanks, Pete," Jessica said. She slipped into the truck, tugging at her little black skirt, then stretched her long legs under the dash. The rotund doorman tipped his hat and closed the door.

Tom cleared his throat. "Good morning."

Jessica turned her bright blue gaze on him. Her sweet lips

curved in a smile. "Good morning."

He could only fathom to what degree his face heralded his lovesick state. Not that Jessica would notice. They were "best friends." And best friends weren't supposed to fall in love with one another. Some unspoken law of ethics dictated he keep his mouth shut—unless he was prepared to risk losing her forever. And he wasn't.

Reaching across the seat, Jess wrapped her pretty tapered fingers around his upper arm. "Thanks for doing this for me, Tom." She tilted her head. Her thick, dark hair fell forward over one shoulder. "The good news is I've run out of single friends." Her musical laugh rippled over him. "This should be our last trip for a fitting."

"No problem." Tom slid the gearshift into drive. Any normal male would be relieved to be let off the hook. But, barring her driving phobia, Jess never asked him to step in as her knight in shining armor. He'd volunteered—heart and soul.

"I have the directions." Jess riffled through her soft leather purse. Her clean orange-vanilla scent filled the cab, making its way to his heart. She unfolded several scraps of paper, clucking her tongue, mumbling about having to get organized.

A strong sense of déjà vu hit him. Tom smiled. "The shop is in Queens, right?" He surveyed the traffic on York Avenue, bottled up as far as his eyes could see.

"Yes, Queens—found it!" Jess ran her finger under the black lettering on the page. "The Fifty-ninth Street bridge, of course."

"I'd better try Second Avenue." Tom gave her a sidelong glance. "Do you want to go for breakfast after the fitting?"

Jess bit her lip, eyes narrowed. "I don't know if we'll have time. The new assistant chef didn't work out." She groaned. "Back to working on Saturdays until I find a replacement."

A familiar pinch of disappointment clenched his stomach. "What time do you have to be in Flavors today?" Skimming around a taxi to get to the corner, Tom rolled up the window to block out the sound of the cursing cabbie.

"Around eleven or—ha!" Jess tossed the directions on the seat beside her. She waved around the papers in her other hand. "I forgot I had these with me. Perfect! I need your help."

Tom smiled. *Lord, let her always need me.* "What is it?" A short silence hung between them. From his peripheral vision, he felt her scrutinizing him. "Jess? What—"

"I–I need to find my glasses." She dug inside her purse. "By the way, how did things work out for you with the blind date on Wednesday?"

"Must you ask?" He unzipped his jacket and extended his arm toward her. "You want to help me out of this?" Blind dates weren't meant for people already in love. He had to hand it to Frank. He'd introduced him to quite a few beautiful, intelligent, Christian women. Only he never got past comparing them to Jessica. This was bordering on mental illness. He had to either play his hand and risk losing her or go on being her best buddy for the rest of his life. He sighed. The latter was so much safer.

"Of course I have to ask. It's my job as your nosy friend. What was she like?" Jess tugged at his cuff, then leaned toward him till her breath feathered his face. He could turn to her now. Kiss her— "She was really nice. We just didn't—"

"Click?" Jess peeled off his jacket and squeezed his upper arm. "Have you been working out at the gym behind my back?"

"Nah, I'm just a late bloomer." He could imagine himself later today, digesting her words, letting them feed into his undying hope.

Jess laughed, folded his jacket, and set it on the seat between them. "Sorry the blind date didn't fly." She sighed. "Do you think there's something wrong with us, Tom?"

Oh, yeah, there was definitely something wrong with him. "How so?"

"Well, why are we both still single at thirty-two?" Jess pulled out her glasses and tossed her bag on the seat.

He had the answer to this one. He buried it, cleared his throat. "Maybe we shouldn't have dropped out of the singles' group at church." Maybe if he had never laid eyes on Jessica—

"Oh, Tom, please!" Jess tore off her glasses. "After awhile we were parenting the singles. Remember? They started coming to us for advice like we were two senior citizens."

Laughing, Tom eased the truck onto the bridge. "We have to wait for God's perfect timing. That's all." He glanced across at the Manhattan skyline, the sun glinting off the Empire State Building. "Gorgeous day."

Jess turned. Her clear blue gaze locked on his, snuffing any lingering regret of missing out on "the blind date from heaven" and the Bronx Zoo.

"That's easy for you to say, 'God's perfect timing.' Your biological clock isn't ticking. My job keeps me too busy to socialize. I think I'll try another route."

Battling against the dread curling around his heart, he raked his mind for a way to keep her from taking a new route to finding Mr. Right. "Don't let fear make you run out and do anything stupid." Great! Perfect response.

"Thanks for your vote of confidence." Jess slipped on her glasses, smoothed out the papers in her hand, and readied her pen. "Will you help me fill out this questionnaire, or what?"

"What is that? Another insurance form?" Tom smirked. "For a Scrabble pro, you sure let those forms trip you up." He pulled into the right lane to prepare to exit the bridge. Jess bit her lip, her thick, dark lashes shielding her exquisite eyes. Tom groaned. "Okay, I know that look. What's going on?"

She grinned. "I think I'm going to take Marilyn's route."

His breath stopped in his lungs. "You're not serious?" He forced the words past the dull ache in his throat. Jutting the wheel right, he exited into Queens.

"Well, you're acting as if I slapped your face or something." Jess picked up her purse and stuffed the papers back into her bag.

Talk about misreading signs. If she were willing to go to this extreme, he didn't even qualify for the running. Making a sharp right into a gas station, he stepped on the brakes and threw the gearshift into park.

"What are you doing?" Jess stared at him.

Tom rolled down the window, clicked off the engine, then turned to the attendant. "Fill her up, please." With his hands in a white-knuckled grip on the steering wheel, he turned to face her. "You're talking about an online dating service. Isn't that what Marilyn—"

"A *Christian* online dating service. But forget I ever mentioned it." Jess crossed her arms over her midsection. "Men don't understand these things anyway."

Nodding, he tried to steady his breaths. "Men understand these things all too well. Why don't you take out an ad in *Newsday* while you're at it?"

Jess tossed him a sarcastic grin. "Well, things turned out great for Marilyn. That's how she met her minister husband, and two kids later, she's looking pretty happy from this side of the fence."

"Okay, so it worked out for Marilyn. But if you look at this statistically—"

"See—that's your problem." Jess bristled. "You're letting your mathematical mind take over. Love isn't some perfect formula." She shrugged. "If you choose to look at it statistically—the glass half-empty—that's your prerogative. But I intend to go for it."

"I'm a financial advisor, not a mathematician." Tom handed his credit card to the gas station attendant. "And those papers"—he gestured at her purse with his chin—"what are they?" He knew. He had to hear it with his own ears. Maybe it would knock enough sense into him to know it was time to abandon ship.

Jess swiped her purse off the seat. "It's the Love Online questionnaire." Smiling, she pulled out the papers. "C'mon, Tom. You're the only one I trust to help me fill them out. You see me objectively, but through a man's eyes. You know?"

Objectively? He hadn't been objective since the day Jessica slipped into the desk in front of his, junior year, Manhattan Christian High School. She'd turned, smiled, and asked if he had an extra pen. With his lips pressed tight to hide his braces, he handed her his pen and fell in love straight away.

Tom signed the credit card slip, passed it to the attendant, and restarted the engine. He looked down at the directions to the bridal shop. Perfect. Half a mile and they'd be there. Then the fitting. Then the drive back. And then, if it took a week of praying and fasting, he'd knock every thought of Jessica Stewart out of his thick skull.

🍂

Jessica tapped her foot in time with her growing agitation. A "late bloomer," indeed! All six-foot-one of Tom couldn't walk into Flavors anymore without at least one of the young waitresses swooning over or inquiring about him. Though she harbored the secret dread of losing the security of their friendship, at least she kept her angst to herself. They both knew the day would come when they'd break their teenage vow of "best friends forever." A spouse would take precedence in their lives. The thought made her hyperventilate, so she forced it away. Jess scanned the questionnaire. "You might want to try this yourself."

"No, thanks." Tom punched the ON button on the CD. He immediately started humming—his habit when pushed to his limits.

Jess took in a deep breath. "Tom, I know you're looking out for me, but—"

"And I know"—he shot her a glance, his dark eyes blazing—"nobody can stop you when you've got your heart set on something." He raked a hand through his light-brown hair, now gold-flecked from the sun, then pushed the OFF button on the CD player. "You're liable to run into Jack the Ripper on one of those Internet—"

Jess burst into laughter. A scowl crossed Tom's handsome face. She covered her mouth with her hand. "Sorry." A muscle in his clamped jaw flicked, tamping down any residual humor.

"I can only imagine the idiotic questions." Tom hit the turn signal, shaking his head. "Really profound stuff like 'What's your favorite color?'"

Jess bit back a grin. She scanned the page, skipping the idiotic stuff. "Actually most of the questions are much deeper than that." She pushed her glasses up to the bridge of her nose. "How about this one? 'Are you willing to relocate?'"

Tom slowed the truck and pulled into a spot. "We're here."

Jess glanced up at Queens' Bridal Emporium, then returned her gaze to the questionnaire. "See—this is why I need your help. Am I willing to relocate?"

With a snort, Tom leaned hard against the seat and folded his arms. "I have no idea, Jess. I wouldn't think so, but then I never thought you'd resort to husband hunting on the Internet." His serious gaze met hers, sending a shudder of embarrassment up her spine.

Jessica tilted her chin. "I guess we should go in."

"I'd rather stay in the car." Tom reclined the seat back.

Biting the inside of her lip, Jess glared at him. "You always come in with me." Tom didn't budge. Sixteen years of friendship, and suddenly she didn't know the man beside her. "Fine, then." She tossed the questionnaire aside, grabbed her purse, and unclipped the seat belt. She flicked another glance his way. Tom stared out the side window. Regret washed through her, landing in the pit of her stomach. She had the sense she'd crossed an invisible boundary that threatened their friendship and changed things forever.

Jess flipped back the door handle. "I shouldn't be too long." She stepped out of the truck. She could stop the train wreck now. Tell Tom the Internet dating brainchild had been borne of her desperation to find a Christian husband. Tell him her destiny would be better left to God's timing after all. But something deep inside told her it was too late to backpedal.

Tom tucked his hands behind his head and gave her a sideways glance. "You're going to be late for your fitting, Jess."

She hopped back into the truck and slammed the door. "I'm not in the mood anymore."

The soft buzz of the electric seat could've been a jackhammer in her ears. Sitting in an upright position, Tom turned the key in the ignition. No negotiating. No talking sense into her. *Where's the Tom I know?* He shifted into drive, and either the truck, or her heart, lurched.

Jess swallowed hard. Her eyes burned. She straightened her shoulders and stared out her side window. No way would she succumb to tears. She'd done nothing wrong. Tom's overprotective attitude bordered on paranoia.

Jessica's stomach sank as Tom headed back toward the bridge. She'd have to make this hike into Queens all over again—most likely without her best friend. She'd grown far too dependent on him, not only for car rides, but also for his strong shoulder. Only Tom got to see the needy side of the chic, savvy, Manhattan chef. Jess cleared her throat and tilted her chin. "I don't know what you're so angry about."

"I wouldn't say I'm angry." Tom cupped his hand over the back of his neck, tipping his head side to side. "You certainly don't need my permission to meet guys online."

His words jabbed her stomach, compelling her to test them. "So then will you help me with the questionnaire?"

Tom glanced at her and shrugged. "Sure. Why not?"

Jess tried to smile, but his bland tone, his sudden change of heart, froze her face. "After all, who, besides God, knows me better than you, Tom?"

"Nobody, Jess." Tom nodded slowly. "Nobody."

two

Tom reread the memo from Elliot Martin and set it aside. He returned his attention to the folder on his desk. His boss's offer of a transfer to the West Coast would mean a promotion, a salary increase, and lots of perks.

Who was he kidding? The lure wasn't in the money and the perks. Leaving New York would be the best way to say good-bye to Jessica. He couldn't rely on willpower alone to keep away from her. Was there really any use in staying?

Closing his eyes, Tom sent up a silent prayer. *Show me if this is what You want, Lord, because right now this move is what I need.*

"Knock, knock."

Tom glanced up to see Frank Dante peering around the door. "Hi, come on in," he said, pushing back from his desk. He stood and stretched the kinks out of his back. "I could use a break from this Randolph account."

Frank closed the door and shuffled across the plush green carpet. "Well?" He smiled, arms outstretched. "How was your weekend?"

Tom shrugged. "Not bad." *Miserable.* He slipped his hands into his pockets. "Long story." Not true exactly. Jessica's news had been sudden and crushing. She was moving on. Perhaps it was time for him to do the same. He scanned the transfer agreement again.

"Something tells me"—Frank sank into the chair in front of the desk—"you're sorry you didn't take me up on the zoo with Lovely Lana."

"Nah." He caught Frank's leery look. "Well, maybe." Five

years of a trusting friendship didn't tempt him to confide he'd actually helped Jess fill out the dating questionnaire. He might as well have given her a reference, if not his blessing. But discouragement motivated him to help her make the quickest exit out of his life. "Let's just say things didn't work out as I expected."

Frank flipped his necktie Groucho Marx–style. "Things have not been working out as you expected—for how long?" He shifted lazily in the leather armchair. "Okay, Jessica used to sit in front of you in grade school, but get over it already."

"High school, junior year," Tom countered, sounding pitiful in his own ears.

"Whatever." Frank sighed. "Look—I'm on your side, but what are you waiting for?"

"A miracle." Or maybe a few more lingering looks from Jessica. Why the looks when she thought she needed a dating service to find the man of her dreams? Tom dropped into his swivel chair and drew in a breath. "You know, sometimes I envy you."

Raking his fingers through his cropped, black hair, Frank smirked. "I'm the bomb."

Tom gave a mild snort. "I'll give you this much—you have a load of female friends, and you never get stuck on any of them. Kudos."

"Hey, I like being a bachelor." Frank wriggled his dark brows. "You, on the other hand, want to be married. Nothing wrong with that, except you've got a thing for one woman."

Tom nodded. "Right." The thing he had for Jessica would have to die a sudden death. He'd nearly forgotten that as he listened to her sing a solo in church Sunday, her face waxing angelic. His heart clenched at the memory.

"Two of the administrative assistants out there"—Frank

jerked his thumb toward the door—"would love to go out with you. Why don't you—"

"Now she's got it in her head she'll find a Christian husband on the Internet." A cold knot tightened in his chest. Since Saturday in Flavors, going over the questionnaire with her between sips of cappuccino, he'd tried to pray it away—force it out of his mind. Speaking the words disheartened him all over again.

"Jessica's looking for a husband on the Internet?" The shock in Frank's voice brought him an odd sense of relief. So he wasn't the only one to think the idea of it insane. "Things are going from bad to worse, Buddy."

"You're right." Bad to worse. Flipping open the file on his desk, Tom shook his head. The few times he did date, he'd done it more as a favor to Frank. Not surprisingly, his colleague attracted women who wanted to double date. Maybe Frank's slick demeanor elicited a safety-in-numbers response. Tom suppressed a grin at the errant thought.

"Last you told me, Jess was off dating. Career first and all that. When did marriage enter the picture?"

"I guess she's achieved everything she's ever wanted career-wise. I'm happy for her. But now," he said with a shrug, "she says her 'biological clock is ticking.' " Drumming his fingers on the desktop, Tom switched his gaze to the window and stared at the skyscraper across the way. "Strange this should come up now. I had every intention of telling Jess how I felt about her this weekend. God's timing, I guess."

"Man, that's rough." Frank rose to his feet and crossed his arms. Tom watched him pacing a small section of carpet. His familiar posture meant a bright idea was brewing, probably one he could live without. "Why don't you join the Christian dating service yourself?" He raised a hand to forestall a response. "*You* actually care if a woman has a good personality." Frank chuckled. "Sorry. I couldn't resist."

Tom grimaced. Leaning back in his chair, he weighed the proposition he'd solidly rejected when Jess presented it to him. "What kind of women could I expect to meet on there?"

Frank cleared his throat. "I think you've just insulted Jessica."

Tom managed a smile. If he were going for the transfer to California, there was no sense starting up a relationship in New York. Though it wouldn't kill him to interact with some like-minded females. Maybe it would be the elixir he needed to put Jessica out of his mind once and for all.

Frank pushed back his shirt cuff and glanced at his watch. "Whoa! Got to get back to work." He strode to the door and turned. "I'm going to the gym at six. Want to catch up with me?"

"Yeah, sure, see you later." The door snapped shut. Tom resumed drumming his fingers. Maybe he'd meet other professional Christians online—women like Jess who had no time to socialize. "Yeah, maybe Jessica's clone."

Tom shook his head and picked up his pen. Frank nailed it. Bad to worse.

❧

Juggling three tubs of ice cream, Jess navigated the creaky wooden stairs from the pantry into the kitchen. She dropped the slippery containers onto the counter and heaved a sigh.

"How are you, Chef?"

Jess glanced up to see Juan standing at the opposite end of the long table, eyeing one of his heavenly confectionery creations. If anybody loved his work as much as she did, it had to be the pastry chef. "Hi, there. When did you get in?"

"About ten minutes ago," Juan said, slathering frosting on the chocolate decadence cake. "It's six o'clock. You leaving?"

"Nope." Jess brushed her hands against her white apron. "I've got to pull another double till we find a new sous chef.

Martha quit on your day off." She scanned the slip of paper hanging from the peg above the stove, grabbed a frying pan, and set it on the flame.

"You better tell boss-man to get somebody quick. With the busy season coming"—Juan glanced up from his master-piece—"you work too hard."

"Yeah, well—" Double shifts weren't so bad when all you had to go home to was a parakeet and a couple of goldfish. Tom hadn't phoned in four days. A record. "You know, Juan—men are strange."

"We're strange?" He grunted.

"Sorry." Jess scooped butter into the pan. Juan had enough problems on the home front to know better than to make the offhand remark. "Just thinking out loud." If Tom was too irri-tated to phone her and was worried about Jack the Ripper, why the pleasantness when he'd helped her fill out the ques-tionnaire? Why help her at all?

Tossing shrimp into the pan, Jess went to the refrigerator for the provolone. After Tom's warnings, she hadn't joined the dating service after all. But if Tom persisted in being unreasonable and stubborn, she wouldn't tell him she had qualms about signing up.

Dora pushed through the swinging doors in her customary breathless fashion. She slapped a receipt on the peg. "Hey, your friend is out there."

Jess closed the fridge door and blinked. "Which friend?"

"The hunk." Dora's munchkin laugh echoed through the kitchen. "Tom Winters."

Delight hit the pit of her stomach, working its way to her face in the form of a smile. She'd missed him more than she cared to admit. "Oh, right, Tom." Her smile faded. He could at least have phoned to let her know he'd be in.

"Ay, caramba!"

Scowling, Jess switched her gaze to Juan. Balancing a cake

platter in each hand, he gestured with his chin to the stove. Dora screeched.

Jess pivoted just as the smoke alarm clanged in her ears. "Yikes!" She lurched forward, yanked the pan off the range, and tossed it into the sink. "What's the matter with me?"

Juan set down the cakes, picked up the broom, and poked its handle at the ceiling alarm. He jammed the stick into the button, restoring the kitchen to silence.

"I'll tell everybody false alarm." Dora dashed through the doors before Jess had a chance to snag her back. All she needed was Dora telling customers *not* to panic.

"Oh, Juan." Jess grabbed a clean pan. Stupidly, she felt on the verge of tears.

"I told you, you're working too hard." After opening the side door, he eased up beside her and began cleaning up the ashy remains.

"Yes, that must be it." Layering cheese atop a crock of onion soup, Jess slid the bowl into the toaster oven. She glanced into the small wall mirror. *What a tired mess!* She flicked a sideways glance at Juan, who was scrubbing the burnt pan.

Making her way to the doors, she slipped out of the kitchen quietly. All she wanted was a sneak peek at Tom without his detecting her. She strode forward about ten paces and halted behind a wide pillar. From this vantage point, she'd be able to catch a glimpse of Tom's favorite table. She peered around the pole like a kid playing hide-and-seek.

"What are you doing?"

Jess spun and released a soft gasp. "Nothing!"

Tom tilted his head, his dark eyes narrowed. "I heard the alarm. You okay?"

Clamping her hands behind her back, she straightened. "Yes, of course. A little mishap, but—"

"When you have a minute"—Tom smiled, sending a

whirly-twirly to her stomach—"could you stop by my table?"

Why was she thinking whirly-twirly about her best friend? More than a little dread washed through her. Jess pulled in a deep breath. "Sure. Business or pleasure?"

"Business." Tom winked. "Make me look good."

"Right." Pressing her hand flat against the pillar, she watched him walk away, tall and handsome in his dark suit. A distant bell rang in her head. *The alarm!* Pivoting, she ran toward the kitchen, banged through the doors, and clamped both of her hands to her face.

Speaking Spanish furiously, Juan was taking aim at the alarm with the broom handle again.

Jess flew to the toaster oven, tears spilling down her face.

"I got it already," Juan called.

Staring down at the blackened cheese on the soup crock, she dabbed her cheeks with the back of her hand. She could easily rip off her chef's uniform, jump into her street clothes, and run out the back door. And keep on running. Trade in all of this for—for what? Since marriage proposals weren't plentiful, did she even have options? She didn't know how to do anything but cook, and judging by the amount of black in her kitchen, she was beginning to doubt that.

She shook her head. Her father had worked double shifts all her life to ensure she had the best education. He didn't want her to become the damsel in distress after he was gone. *If you're looking down from heaven, Daddy, I'm sorry for acting so 'girly-girl' under stress. It's not what you taught me.*

More tears came unabated, running hot and zigzagging down her face. Grasping the edge of the counter, Jess took in deep breaths. *I can do this.* She moved to the refrigerator.

This job was everything she'd ever wanted. She'd practically broken her back to become the top chef at one of Manhattan's best restaurants, and she wasn't about to blow it all in one emotional outburst. Her gaze skipped over Juan's sympathetic smile. She grabbed another pan.

Assembling each dish methodically, her thoughts returned to Tom. He was virtually the only man alive who knew the weak and needy Jessica. It was far too dangerous to be thinking of Tom in terms of whirly-twirlies. That would never do. She could show her best friend that side of her, but never the man she intended to marry. Her father was right—it was fine to want a man, but not to need one.

And she needed Tom.

She'd have to put a lid on whatever sparked the wild attraction in the dining room. Four days without speaking to him probably accounted for overreacting at the sight of him.

"Juan, I'll take the desserts out to Tom's table."

Spooning an extra dollop of heavy cream on the brownie, Juan pushed the plate toward her. "Finished."

"Beautiful." Jess smiled. She picked up the tray and walked through the doors. If Tom had bothered to ask her to make him look good, his dinner guests must be important—

Jess stopped a few feet from the table, hesitating to intrude on what appeared to be an intimate exchange between Tom and the beautiful woman sitting beside him. But she tilted her chin, smiled, and approached.

"Jessica." Tom stood, as if surprised to see her in her own place of work.

"Good evening." Jess set down the desserts. "Was everything okay?"

The two older, distinguished gentlemen nodded and smiled. The woman stared at Tom starry-eyed, perhaps hoping he'd do the talking for her.

"This is Heather Webster," Tom said.

She looked like a Heather Webster. A pale, blond beauty

who rode horses in Connecticut. Jess shook her outstretched hand. "Pleased to meet you." After being introduced to Tom's two other guests, she stepped back, only too happy to make a hasty retreat.

"Oh," Heather whispered, "the salmon was a little dry."

Jessica's already shaky smile froze on her face. "Was it? I'm so sorry."

Heather waved her delicate hand. "No big deal, actually." She turned to Tom, a benign smile on her face. "No big deal," she mouthed.

Tom cleared his throat. "Everything I had was delicious."

"Great—well, have a nice rest of the evening." Jess turned and strode quickly toward the kitchen. There was no way she'd permit herself another bout of tears.

"Jess, wait."

She spun toward Tom's voice, finding he had followed her. There was no good reason for her to feel stabbed in the back. But that's precisely how she felt. Like she was losing her grasp on something—her stability or their friendship.

"Sorry about that rude comment. Heather was fine with the dinner while she was eating it." Tom grinned.

"No problem," she fibbed. "I can't be perfect." Everything in her wanted to ask why he hadn't called. She forced back the questions. "By the way, I decided not to join the online dating service."

"You did?" Tom dipped his chin.

Instead of setting their friendship back on course, Tom sounded disappointed. "Well, I–I. . ." She searched for words to recover from her embarrassment. "I'm sure I can find husband material some other way."

"Ah." Tom nodded. "Well, this may sound funny, but I'm going to join."

"Funny?" Jess whispered. "I—"

"We'll talk later. I have to get back to my table."

Funny? In the kitchen, Jess leaned against the table, shaking her head. What a kick in the shins. Now she would join Love Online if it were the last thing she did! And looking around her, it hit her that it just might be the last thing she did.

three

Tom popped two slices of bread into the toaster and poured himself a cup of coffee. Yawning, he went to his laptop on the kitchen table and typed in his password. "Curiosity killed the cat," his mom would say. He smiled, then took a long swallow from his cup. The Love Online idea may have started as a means to get Jess out of his mind, but now he was curious about the kind of feedback he'd get. Would he be the most popular guy of the Internet world or the nerd no one contacted?

Scanning his E-mail, Tom grimaced as he counted the messages. Eighteen responses, and he hadn't even posted his mug shot. This endeavor might require more time than he'd bargained for. But at least his world had options where they hadn't existed before.

Opening the first message, he took a few seconds to assimilate his new identity—TCTwo—and how he'd come to decide on it. He never used his middle name, Christopher, but he was born Thomas Christopher Winters II, after all. The long-awaited son after four daughters, his parents thought he was royalty. He shook his head. They meant well, but their decision to retire to Florida turned out for the best all the way around. As far as his family was concerned, Jess was their future daughter-in-law. He wouldn't fare well, having to explain a couple of visits to their house without her.

At the sound of the toaster, Tom returned to the counter. Jess still might be husband hunting, but at least now she wouldn't put herself at risk on the Internet—or so she said when he'd seen her last in Flavors.

Poor Jess, he thought, buttering his toast. She seemed shaken Thursday night. Was it Heather's dry-salmon remark? Jess might be a perfectionist, but he could count on one hand the times he'd seen her cry in sixteen years. And Thursday she'd looked close to tears. She was such an anomaly. She hadn't had a successful date in years, yet never a tear, but one comment on her salmon and she was putty. Perhaps that's why he loved her so. He never knew what to expect.

This month had always been a struggle for her—first Mother's Day, followed by the anniversary of her beloved father's death. He grimaced. He felt like a slug for not being there to help her over the hurdles in May.

Tom gave a grunt, jerked open the refrigerator door, and replaced the butter. As if Jess needed him to make it through life! She'd made it clear he lacked what she required when it came to a lifetime commitment.

Taking his juice and toast to the table, he sat down to read the first E-mail, grateful for the anonymity of the process. No real names, they strongly recommended, just initials or handles. Most members posted photos, but there was truth behind Frank's witty comment. Physical attributes had little to do with being well matched. If physical attraction were the key to compatibility, he and Jess would be celebrating their tenth wedding anniversary. Enough people had referred to them as a "beautiful couple" to make them crack up whenever they heard it.

Tom shoved the thought aside, rested his chin on his fist, and looked at the computer screen.

Dear TCTwo,
I read your profile. My photo and other information are posted on the site. I live on East 34th Street and...

Tom's gaze dropped to the bottom of the message. The

woman signed her real name. "Not smart." He took a bite into the toast and brushed the crumbs off his fingers. He'd have to write and let her know she should be more careful. He closed and saved her E-mail, then opened the next.

No salutation. *I've never done this before, and I'm not desperate to meet men!*

Tom burst out laughing. Wait till he got his hands on Frank for goading him into joining. The more he read of the missive, the more relieved he felt that Jess hadn't subjected herself to this.

Drinking his orange juice, Tom moved on to the third E-mail:

Dear TCTWO,
   If you want to see my personality profile, I'm listed as Lab711. It seems we have a lot in common. I see you're a backgammon pro. Me too! And I can give you a run for your money. I also enjoy jogging, dining out, funny movies, and antiquing.
   I'm in my early thirties, live in Manhattan, and, like you, my career keeps me too busy to socialize on a regular basis. I haven't posted my photo and probably won't, but I'm slender, tall, have dark hair and blue eyes. (If you're thinking Liz Hurley, think again, but I'm attractive on a different level.)

Tom leaned back in his chair and caught his breath. She could've been describing Jess. Shaking his head, he groaned. "None of that stuff." As Frank said, "Get over it already!" He refocused on the remainder of her message.

   More important than looks, hobbies, career, etc., I want to meet a man who loves the Lord and puts Him first in his life. If you're still interested in communicating, I'd like to hear from you.

                                                              Sincerely, L

Raising his brows, Tom pressed the REPLY button. "Okay, Lab-seven-eleven. . ." Her interests and priorities were definitely similar to his. Why not?

Tom crossed his arms while composing a reply in his head, then set his fingers to the keyboard. He didn't have to meet her face-to-face until, and unless, he felt ready, but the sooner he started his journey in a new direction, the better.

At the shrill of the phone, Tom glanced up at the clock and decided to let the machine get it. Instead of the hang-up from a telemarketer he'd anticipated, he heard Heather Webster's soft voice. He stood, went to the living room, and approached the voice machine hesitantly.

"I know it's Saturday," Heather uttered apologetically, "but I'd love it if you could take some time this afternoon to meet with me before I leave town. I need clarity on the finer points of the financial analysis you did for us, and—"

Tom rubbed his hand across his jaw. Pick up? *She's a client. She needs help.* He expelled a breath and grabbed the cordless. "Hello, Heather."

"Wonderful! I caught you in!"

Where else would he be at eight in the morning on his day off? "Yeah, I was planning on a jog in the park, but afterward we can—"

"Sounds tempting. Mind if I join you?"

"On my jog?" Tom cupped his hand to the back of his neck. Business and pleasure were usually a sour mix. He cleared his throat. "I thought you wanted me to look over the reports."

"I do, but I can afford to work off a few extra pounds before we get to it." Heather laughed. "Plus I need your signature on something. It's sort of a recommendation. Long story."

Tom smiled. If only Jess heard the overweight comment coming from rail-thin Heather, she'd say, "She's fishing for compliments." Much as he wanted to give her one, he thought better of baiting his client. "I'm leaving in about fifteen minutes." That should discourage her.

"Sounds good. I'm staying at the Beverly, a couple of blocks from you if I'm reading your business card correctly."

Great! Tom dragged his hand through his hair. No polite way to squirm out of it. "I'll be waiting downstairs then."

After hanging up, he went to the kitchen and snapped off the computer. Out of necessity, his new life would have to be put on hold for awhile longer.

❧

"Get your feet off that sofa right now!" Marilyn sprinted around the wooden coffee table while her three year old skillfully dodged her grasping hand.

Jess pressed her fingers to her lips to hide her grin from the precocious toddler. "It's an old sofa, Marilyn. Don't worry about it."

"He has to learn to listen," she said between gasps. With her curly blond hair popping loose from her ponytail holder, Marilyn scooped her chubby son under one arm and dropped to the sofa. "On my lap, Mister, till you learn to behave." She puffed out a breath. "So what's that you were saying about your biological clock?"

Jess laughed. "What a workout." Sitting in the armchair across from her closest female friend, she tucked her legs under her and smiled at Nathan—red-faced and squirming his protest. "I was saying I never wanted marriage and children more than I do right now."

Brushing her fingers through Nathan's dark hair, Marilyn rocked him into a slightly calmer state. "You really did it, huh?" She shook her head, her curls bobbing. "I'd never figure you for online dating. You're the one who always had men chasing after you goo-goo eyed."

Jess waved her hand. "That means nothing—you know that. Unfortunately, no one I want to catch me ever chases me."

"Don't be so hasty, Girl." Marilyn eased Nathan off her lap

and onto the sofa and continued stroking his hair. "Oh, please take a nap. That'll be two down." Her big brown eyes motioned toward her younger son, Paul, curled up on a blanket on the carpet, his thumb working in his mouth. "You had options, Jess. You always had options."

"Not with my dad." Jess laughed, but a familiar stab of mixed emotion accompanied the mention of her father. "I loved Daddy so much, but I'll always wonder what he was trying to protect me from. Some of his advice made me scared to walk out the door in the morning."

"Double duty." Marilyn tilted her head thoughtfully. "I saw it a lot when I was teaching. One parent struggling to be both. Without your mother around—"

Jess gave a mild snort. "What mother? Unless you count the fact that she gave birth to me." She shrugged. There was no sense living in the land of regrets. "Anyway, you had options too."

Marilyn smirked. "Let's put it this way: I never had a *friend* like Tom Winters squiring me around town."

Jess shook her head. "You know Tom and I are friends. For real, just friends."

Marilyn rolled her gaze heavenward. "If you say so."

"Okay, you've managed to do it again." Jess folded her arms. "You're making me feel guilty—as if I'm hiding something, and I'm not."

"That's good news," she shot back too cheerfully. "Just friends means it won't phase you in the least when you see Tom with another woman, right?"

Jess fluffed her long hair and switched her gaze to the living room window. "You mean jealousy?" What was that ugly twinge she felt when she saw Heather Webster sitting beside Tom, her eyes flashing interest? "I have no right to be jealous. I'll be happy for Tom when he meets the right woman. As long as he chooses well. That's part of my job as his friend, to protect him, you know." She gave Marilyn a sideways glance, preferring not to meet her doubtful grin head-on. "Why doesn't anybody get it that men and women can be friends?"

Marilyn lifted her hands in surrender. "Okay, I confess—I don't get it." She leaned back against the cushions, grabbed a pillow, and hugged it to her. "You guys spend every free waking moment together—go to movies, dinner, even grab lunch when you can squeeze it in. You sit side-by-side in church like all the married couples. And, worst of all, you laugh at each other's stupid jokes—humor nobody else understands."

"Oh, come on!" Jess tried, unsuccessfully, to restrain a smile. "Tom is funny, isn't he?"

"There!" Marilyn pointed an accusing finger. "See! You can't even talk about him without your face lighting up."

"Oh, please." Jess got to her feet. "I'll get us some tea." She started toward the kitchen. "I made chocolate mousse," she said with her back to her friend.

"Yeah, that's right. Ignore me."

Standing at the counter and grateful to be out from under Marilyn's probing gaze, she tried to untangle fact from fiction. She loved Tom. No doubt about it. But that didn't mean they should be setting a marriage date. Not that Tom had ever asked. And not that she'd say yes. Crazy! Love and in love were two entirely different emotions.

Jess took the dessert bowls from the refrigerator. Marilyn had a way of making her question her own reality. She'd do well to keep in mind that her dear friend had a flair for the dramatic at times. "Are you watching your waistline again?" she called, whipped cream canister poised over the dessert.

"No, I'm pregnant."

Very funny. Paul wasn't even walking yet. Jess squirted cream on the mousse, set the sugar bowl, spoons, teacups, and napkins on the tray, and carried it out into the living room. "Pregnant." She placed the serving tray on the oval table. "You're a regular comedienne today."

"What?" Staring, straight-faced, Marilyn picked up a bowl and spoon. "I'm pregnant. I'm not kidding."

Jess dropped to the carpet and scooted closer to the coffee table. She fought back the despair tearing at her heart. Not only was she always the bridesmaid, but she was also always the aunt. Never the mother. Was there anyone for her? "Congratulations. That's great. It really is."

"I'm sorry." Sliding to the edge of the sofa, Marilyn dipped the spoon into the mousse. "This looks positively sinful."

"Sorry? For what?" Jess took a sip of tea. Her friend could read her too well. She should know better than to try to fool Marilyn—or Tom.

"Delicious." Marilyn closed her eyes and licked her lips.

"I'm thrilled for you. It's just that a ridiculous thought struck me. I'll never catch up now." Jess laughed. "Talk about putting the horse before the cart."

"If you haven't met Mr. Right already, you will."

Spooning the dessert into her mouth, she chose not to acknowledge Marilyn's not-so-veiled reference to Tom. "Why don't we go for a walk in Central Park when we're through? Maybe stop by the zoo with the kids?"

"Great idea." Marilyn averted her gaze to Nathan's sleeping form. "I miss Keith when he goes off to these conferences."

"Not easy being a minister's wife, I guess. But God sure is blessing you for the sacrifices you make. Look at these gorgeous kids." Her life, by comparison, seemed empty and shallow. "And to think—it all started with dating online."

Scraping the bottom of the dessert bowl, Marilyn's eyes widened. "Uh-uh! Surely you've forgotten my *Twilight Zone* experiences before I met Keith!"

"Well, there were a few rotten apples in the bunch, but—"

"What? A few?" Marilyn set aside her cup and wriggled her fingers. "Eight in a row!"

Jess bit her lip. She'd made the decision to quit at five. Five online disaster dates and she'd throw in the towel. "Yes, I do remember now. There was the guy who took you to the expensive restaurant, didn't let you know till the check came that—"

" "I had to pay my own way," Marilyn said nodding. "His last name was Singer—just in case he's still out there. You'll want to avoid him like the plague."

"I'll say." Memories of Marilyn's ordeals tumbled through her mind. "What about the guy who asked you what he should do about his stinky feet problem?" Jess shuddered.

Marilyn laughed so loud that Nathan jumped. "Yeah, and he went into so much detail that"—her shoulders shook with laughter—"I lost my appetite." Wiping a tear from her eye, she held up her hand and took a breath. "I'm going to have to pray none of this happens to you, dear friend. You're such a delicate flower compared to me."

"I need all the prayer I can get." Jess hastened to her feet, leaving but a spoonful of her dessert untouched. She'd never been sensitive, but lately. . . "I'll clean up, and then we'll get going."

"I bet it's my fault"—Marilyn stood and stretched—"that you missed your jog in the park with Tom this morning."

"Actually, Tom didn't call to ask." Jess glanced at her watch. "It's almost ten, and he leaves early. It's not your fault in any case." She turned and padded into the kitchen.

She had made a point of trying to convince Marilyn that she and Tom were just friends, but the tumult in her heart told her she missed Tom more than any friend should. Rinsing the dishes, Jess turned at the sound of approaching footsteps.

"Are you sure you're up to running around Central Park with two screaming kids?" Marilyn's eyes narrowed. "Or are you just feeling sorry for me?"

Jess laughed. "Aren't you the pitiful one?" She shook her head. "Believe it or not, I want to go to the Central Park Zoo with two screaming kids."

And if Tom happened to be there, all the better. She wouldn't mind a bit the sight of the easy smile she'd come to depend on whenever she saw him.

Though despite Marilyn's inferences, a dating relationship would destroy their solid-like-a-rock friendship. It wasn't as if she hadn't witnessed the carnage of other male-female friendships gone down the tubes in the name of love.

Jess dried her hands on the dish towel. She could never afford to lose Tom as a friend. In reality, Tom was the only family she had left. But why was he avoiding her?

four

Tom rounded the curve toward the finish line, his Nikes flapping hard against the pavement. He decelerated slowly, leaned forward, and clasped his hands to his knees. So much for showing off to keep pace with stick-thin, fresh-out-of-grad-school Heather. Straightening, he took a deep breath.

Heather fake-punched him in the arm. "That was quite a workout." Jogging in place with her hands on her hips, she laughed. Barely a drop of sweat tarnished the smooth terrain of her forehead.

Tom uncapped his water bottle. *Quite a workout.* Half the speed and distance would've sent him and Jessica slumping to the grass in a heap. After glugging a long drink of water, he scanned the busy park.

In-line skaters sped in impatient zigzags around leisurely strolling pedestrians. A smile tugged at his mouth. He and Jess liked to make a game of guessing which were tourists and which couples were dating or married. He could just hear Jess's comments about Heather and her perfectly coordinated running outfit. He stifled a grin and pushed the thought aside.

"I'm going back to my place." Tom grabbed the corners of the towel around his neck and swabbed his face. He glanced at his watch. "How about we meet up in an hour?"

Heather's lips twitched in an expression between wounded and determined. "I thought we could get right to it."

Tom nodded. If only he had a clue what she was talking about. He dropped to the park bench, his rapid pulse reminding him of the perils of chasing a twenty-something around the park. He made a mental note to add a comment to his Love Online profile: Only fast walkers need apply.

Heather tilted her blond head. "Well?"

Apparently there was a correct response, but he'd forgotten the question. "What do you want to do?" Pulling in another breath, he rested his elbows on his thighs and studied the black tar path. "That *was* quite a workout."

Heather propped herself beside him, crossed her bare legs, and swung her pink-and-white–sneakered foot back and forth. Wearing white shorts and a sleeveless tennis blouse, she appeared oddly underdressed, considering the snappy north wind coming off the river. But enough with the cynicism—and the comparisons.

"I thought we'd grab brunch in the park." Heather poked her face into his line of vision. "I don't have to go back to the hotel for the paperwork. Everything I want to discuss with you is in here." She pointed her pink manicured nail to her head.

No doubt Heather's mind rivaled her quick sprint, or she wouldn't be representing Goldman Enterprises. He touched his back pocket. Good thing he had the foresight to carry his wallet. "What are you in the mood to eat?"

She smoothed her hand over her flat stomach. "Nothing fattening." A small worry line formed between her brows, creasing her flawless skin. "You're looking sort of flushed."

"Am I?" Tom's pulse kicked up. No, he wouldn't indulge in a bout of hypochondria and lose a potential multimillion-dollar account. "I'm great." He got to his feet, if only to prove he could.

Heather sprang up, then looped her arm through his. Before he could conjure up a polite way to extricate himself from her iron grip, they were walking arm-in-arm. "There's a café in the park. We could sit outside." Tom slipped his hands into the pockets of his black jogging pants. Instead of loosening her grip, Heather moved in closer, then coquettishly pulled away a bit.

He had to admit she was charming. If only his mind—and his heart—would let go of Jess. There had to be something wrong with a man who wanted to play hero to a woman who looked beyond him to find a husband.

"Sounds good then," Heather said, lifting her smiling face up to his. "I'm loving New York. This is my second time here, but the first was strictly business."

This is too, Tom wanted to counter. Somehow he'd gotten roped into this situation this morning, but even pretty Heather couldn't change his mind about mixing business with pleasure.

"I think you should know"—Heather bit her lip, arching her brows—"I'm considering moving to New York."

"Why?" Tom smiled in an effort to cover the disappointment in his voice. "I mean, I thought you loved Boston. Why New York?"

"I don't know. Maybe it's the energy here." Heather looked skyward. "Even the traffic, the noises, all the craziness." Squeezing his arm, she laughed. "And the people. Thanks to you, I had an unforgettable week."

"You're welcome, but—" The entertainment came with his job description. Any savvy businesswoman should know that. "What about your career at Goldman?" Passing the frankfurter stand, Tom's stomach grumbled at the scent of boiling hot dogs wafting on the air. He acknowledged the vendor with a wave. "Hey, Chuck."

"Two with sauerkraut?" Chuck's gaze darted to Heather, but the ex-Vietnam vet had been around the park too long to let his face give away any questions. He had to be wondering what happened to "Sunshine"—his pet name for Jess.

"No, not today," Tom said, feeling his companion straining at his side. He gave her a sidelong glance and headed toward the café, the burden of what to do with Heather growing with every step.

"I called my boss last night, and this is the part I was telling you about on the phone. He wants to open a New York office. He'll let me head the place, as long as I get a couple of our big clients to give me their seal of approval."

Tom reeled in his scattered thoughts. "So you're serious about a transfer?"

"Yes." Heather's smile seemed to beg for some sign of encouragement from him. "If he opens the Manhattan branch, can I count on your recommendation?"

"Sure." Tom frowned. "But have you given this a lot of thought?" He had every inclination to suggest she pray on the matter, but he didn't sense a spiritual bent in her. Just one more thing he loved about Jess. A perfect day was spreading a blanket on the grass, opening their Bibles, and unearthing the most astounding spiritual truths over a scrumptious lunch she'd prepared.

"Oh, look!" Heather sucked in a soft gasp and gestured to the wooden sign. "A zoo!"

Oh, no, Lord, please! "The zoo is packed on Saturdays." Tom raked his overtaxed brain to divert her attention. "The restaurant is up ahead."

"Can we go to the zoo?" she pleaded. "After brunch?" Heather's eyes shone up at him from her baby face. Was she flirting? He wouldn't recognize flirting unless a woman hit him over the head, Frank alleged. In Heather's presence, he felt solidly hit over the head.

This was his Saturday. His day off. *Right.* And he'd be toast if Elliot found out he did anything to lose this account. "Sure—if you'd like."

"I'd like."

❧

"If I have to ask you again—" Marilyn knelt beside the

twin stroller. "Do you want me to strap you in?"

Nathan kicked his feet. "Nooo, I said."

"Shh, you're going to wake Paul." Marilyn removed the cellophane wrapper from a lollipop. Nathan grasped it in his dimpled hand. "Now stop leaning forward before you break your neck!" She rose and blew out a long breath. "Want me to take over?"

Jess shook her head. "I like pushing the kids." She smiled at a passerby. Being mistaken for the boys' mommy wasn't so bad either. Only the Lord knew if she'd ever experience the real thing. She leaned over the handlebars. "Want to see the monkeys?"

Nathan popped up and down in his seat, stopping once to eye Marilyn dolefully.

"I guess that means yes." Jess laughed, pushing the stroller uphill and listening to her friend crack peanuts between her teeth. "This is a nice day, Marilyn. Why haven't we done this more often?"

"I don't know. First it was lousy weather; then you working double shifts. I guess we both got too busy. But this summer we'll make a point of—oh, boy."

"What?" Scowling, Jess stopped and examined Marilyn's whitish face. "What? I bet you broke a tooth on one of those stupid peanuts."

"Um. . .not exactly." Marilyn stared down at the spent shells in her cupped hand. "Maybe we've had enough of the zoo today."

"What? We haven't seen the monkeys yet." Jess tried to catch Nathan's attention to assist in her protest, but he was totally absorbed in his red lollipop. Planting her fist on her hip, she shot Marilyn a look. "Okay, what's going on?"

"Let's rest for awhile." Marilyn meandered toward the park bench and lowered herself to the seat.

Jess followed, her heart speeding up. "You're not having

pains or anything, are you?"

"Of course not. I'm only a few months' pregnant." Marilyn snorted a laugh. "Like I'm going to give birth in the middle of Central Park."

Dropping down beside her, Jess felt her stomach pitch. "Something *is* wrong though. Tell me."

Marilyn glanced around, then shook her head. "I'd rather not say."

A brisk wind rustled through the maples. Jess shivered. She scanned the winding trail, now clogged with noisy park-goers. Her gaze settled on a twosome standing in front of a cage, their backs to her. As her brain registered the sight, her breath stopped. It dawned suddenly that her jaw was hanging open.

Closing her mouth, she swallowed past the dryness in her throat, then looked at Marilyn. "It's—it's Tom and. . ." *Heather Webster.*

"Yeah, I know." Marilyn cleared her throat. "I think we should go in the other direction. Take the high road, so to speak."

"Don't be silly!" Jess stood, adjusting her beige chinos, which, she was thankful, concealed her shaky legs. "I have to at least say hello."

Tom was a friend—a free agent. And if she had harbored any suspicion that he ever saw her as a real female, she could safely put the thought to rest right this second. For all their jaunts in the park, they'd never been wrapped in such an intimate embrace. Before her eyes stood the difference between love and in love.

A shiver snaked up her spine, and a teary feeling washed over her. Heather didn't suit Tom at all. Toying with the hem of her sweatshirt, Jess bit her lip. If she said anything to warn Tom away from Heather, she'd sound like a catty, jealous, thirty-two-year-old woman whose chances for marriage and children were fast slipping away. She crossed her arms and looked at Marilyn.

"*You* can go over and say hello." Marilyn wiggled her foot, a habit clearly indicating her distress. "But I'm staying right here."

Straightening her shoulders, Jess assessed the lovebirds again. Heather's tentacles were wrapped around Tom, her adoring gaze glued to his face. Like a fast-deflating balloon, bravado seeped from her limbs. If body language were a barometer, she'd be intruding by acknowledging the two. Opting to remain invisible, Jess swallowed hard and tilted her chin.

Tom had always had a hands-off approach with her. She should be celebrating—instead of standing around pining that she wasn't his type. His brotherly love toward her made for a perfect friendship.

But today she would give anything to know she was somebody's type.

Jess loosened her white-knuckled grip on the stroller handle. Enough of wanting to feed her needy ego. "You know—you're right. Maybe it's best if we leave right now."

Marilyn sprang to her feet. "You don't have to ask twice."

Jess steered the stroller eastward toward the exit. "I would've said hello." To her dismay, her voice quivered. "I just didn't want to make Tom feel uncomfortable."

"Monkeys, monkeys," Nathan whined, as if sensing the growing distance between him and the hairy creatures.

"Not today," Marilyn reasoned in a soft voice. "Who's going to hear the end of this?" She rolled her gaze heavenward. "We'll come back another day and—"

"Wait a second." Jessica stopped in midstep. "This is ridiculous. We're not going to deprive Nathan of seeing the monkeys just because—" She did an about-face, ignoring Marilyn's wide-eyed expression. Just because Tom had forgotten she was alive since he'd met Heather. She let her gaze slide their way. Tom and Blondie were chatting amiably, blissfully unaware of her presence. "We're going to see the monkeys right now, Nathan. Okay?"

"We don't have to do this, Jess. Maybe we shouldn't." Marilyn kept her head down. "Maybe Tom won't see us."

Tom turned slightly, as if to mock her friend's words. His dark gaze met hers. Jess's breath caught as she acknowledged his smile.

Heather twisted around in an apparent effort to scout out what or who had captured Tom's attention.

"Oh, boy," Marilyn whispered.

"Hi, there!" Jess forced cheer into her voice. She took a few bold steps toward the lovebirds.

"Jess." Still smiling, Tom closed the remaining distance between them, the wind tousling his golden-brown hair. "And, Marilyn, how are you?" Tom gestured to his companion. "You remember—"

"Heather." Under the circumstances, a smile would be appropriate. But hard as she tried, none would come. "Nice to see you again."

Heather's mouth lifted in a half-smile. Her gaze immediately returned to Tom's face.

Jess's pulse quickened. Now here was a lady who preferred she didn't exist. But like it or not—she did. And she knew Tom long before Heather sauntered into the picture.

"I'd shake your hand," Marilyn said, though Heather hadn't offered hers. "But—" Holding her palms upward, she produced as evidence the peanut shell residue.

"What have you been up to, Marilyn? I didn't see you in church last Sunday." Tom stooped in front of the stroller. "Hey, Nathan."

"Monkeeees." Nathan shoved his lollipop in front of Tom's nose.

"No, thanks." Tom laughed, ruffled his hair, and stood.

"Paul had a fever last Sunday." Shifting from one foot to the other, Marilyn adjusted her ponytail. "Lord willing, we'll be in church tomorrow."

"Tom." Heather cleared her throat and gave her watch a cursory glance. "Should we get going?"

"Sure, fine."

Jess gritted her teeth. Men could be so blind, but this was ridiculous. Why didn't he just let Heather walk him on a leash?

Tom lifted his hand in a farewell gesture. "Heather's got to catch a plane in a couple of hours, so—"

"We have to be off anyway," Jess interjected, her voice overly merry to her own ears. "Monkeys and all that."

After a quick exchange of good-byes, she left Marilyn at the helm of the stroller. A rush of adrenaline propelled her forward, away from the source of the ache in her heart.

"Wait up." Marilyn's voice came from behind her.

Jess stopped and glanced over her shoulder, past her friend, to Tom's departing form. She could yell, "Wait!" But wait for what? So she could attempt to explain the inexplicable?

A wheezing Marilyn stood beside her. "What was that?"

That was Tom. The man she assumed would be in her life forever. The man she had most likely taken for granted, at least compared to Heather, who looked like she adored him. "What do you mean?"

Marilyn's lips twisted in a sneer. "Get real."

Jess stared straight into her big, questioning eyes and shrugged. "I don't know." She put her hand to her stomach. "I feel as if the Lord just threw me a curve ball."

"Come on—don't be pinning this on God." Marilyn knelt beside the stroller, tucked the blanket around Paul, and handed him a bottle. "Tom is nice looking, isn't he?"

"Who said he wasn't?" Jess bristled. "Regardless"—she waited for Marilyn to meet her gaze—"it looks as if he's met the woman of his dreams."

And my nightmares.

five

Jess emerged from a dark tunnel, her heart drumming hard against her ribs. Sitting forward, she wrestled free of her comforter and reached for the clanging alarm clock on the nightstand.

"Okay, okay," she whispered, snapping down the button. She replaced the clock, then quickly pulled the covers to her neck. This time the dream had left tears on her face and a feeling of dread squarely in the pit of her stomach.

She tuned her senses to the gurgling pigeons inching along her windowsill and the traffic noises ten stories below. Her breaths slowed as blessed reality edged out the residual panic.

Easing her legs over the side of the bed, she sat with her palms flat against the crumpled sheets, squinting at the sun's rays slanting through the venetian blind slats, patterning the wooden floor. She shifted her gaze to the ticking alarm. The white phone stood beside it—silent.

If Tom didn't call by eight o'clock on Sunday mornings, chances were he wouldn't phone at all. *Tom.* What was he doing invading her slumber?

Jess pushed her sleep-tangled hair from her face. Snippets of the nightmare returned. When Tom said, "I love you," a dark, nameless thing, which Tom couldn't see, shook the floor and rattled her free of him. He mistakenly believed she was pushing him away.

But what about Tom's whispered kiss? Jess pressed her fingers to her still-tingling lips. She pulled in another deep breath. No sense probing the recesses of the subconscious,only to rouse sleeping pit bulls.

Jess stood and meandered to the window on rubbery legs. "I'll get to church on my own." She tugged the venetian blind cord to welcome more light into the room, but it lengthened to the floor in a crash. "Great!" She shoved aside the dangling window covering with her bare foot, turned, and strode to the bathroom in the foyer.

Sitting on the edge of the tub, she adjusted the faucets, wriggling her fingers under the gushing water to the tune of her growing impatience. A surge of anger rose in her chest. Only her Christian witness kept her from beating her bare fists against the bathroom wall. She stared at the big gray tile, eyes narrowed. Her neighbor must be enveloped in steam at that moment; he just had to be scheduling his bath times to coincide with hers. Maybe if she had a man around to challenge her landlord, she'd get more consideration.

Jess's shoulders sagged in defeat. She twisted the handles to the off position. "Fine." She wouldn't go to church today. It wasn't as if anybody would miss her anyway. She grabbed her toothbrush, drew a straight line of paste across the bristles, and commenced scrubbing with a vengeance. The Lord promised He'd be with her wherever she went. Today she'd do her devotions at home.

She returned to her bedroom and swiped the Bible off the desk. Marilyn and a few other friends might miss her, but certainly not Tom. Not after what she witnessed in the park yesterday.

Dropping into the chair, she rested the Bible on her lap and opened it to the book of Proverbs. Talk about saintly patience. Jess smoothed her hands over the padded armrests. The lilac material, silky against her skin, dragged her thoughts back to one of their days together.

Tom had spent hours traipsing through antique shops to help her search for the perfect accompaniment to her French country desk. When it came to her whims, Tom's uncomplaining kindness mirrored her father's. And now it seemed they were both out of her reach. The memories threatened to loosen the latch on the door to stored sorrows.

Jess forced her gaze back to the Bible. Best to keep that room bolted. She scanned the words highlighted in yellow, though she knew them by heart.

> *"Ointment and perfume rejoice the heart: so doth the sweetness of a man's friend by hearty counsel."*
> PROVERBS 27:9

The day she'd first read the verse, the Scripture reminded her of Tom's friendship and good counsel. They were all of eighteen when she'd whispered her revelation to Tom. He smiled and said the ointment and perfume part reminded him of her because she smelled so good. Feeling their oats, they had the audacity to giggle in Mr. Baylor's Bible class. The ancient teacher paused, studying them from under gray bristly brows. But Tom had taken full blame for finding humor in the Good Book, which meant a Saturday of his scrubbing the schoolhouse's wooden floors in repentance.

That was Tom. Always trying to save her hide or rescue her. And he'd probably had enough of it. Perhaps Heather wouldn't be so much work. In all likelihood, Tom was ready for a woman who returned his gestures with appreciation.

Jess cleared her throat and readjusted her frame against the carved chair back, but a familiar presence settled over her, prompting her to action more than offering comfort.

There's no sin in praying and reading the Word in my room. Jess flipped through the Bible pages, even knowing the futility of looking busy to impress God. *Why can't I sit here and relax?*

No response.

"Okay, Lord. I don't know why You want me there, but—"

Jess snapped the Bible closed, stood to her feet, and headed for the shower.

Turning the handle to the max, she crossed her arms, waiting for the miracle she knew wouldn't come—hot water. She sighed and, armed with a deep breath, eased one foot into the tub. Her skin bloomed with goose bumps as she hopped in the rest of the way, gasping as the icy spray numbed her skin.

The absurdity of her predicament hit. She got up every morning to do battle with an absentee landlord, which necessitated talking to herself and included a strong desire to pummel her next-door neighbor.

Jess flicked her gaze to the wall. Poor guy. Flipping his key chain as he whistled his way to the elevator, he was most likely oblivious to her existence—let alone the fact that her bath time included plotting the demise of his lease.

"What's wrong with me?" Listening for the Lord's still, small voice, her own dizzying thoughts drowned out whatever He might want to communicate. Part of the answer lay on the surface of her half-frozen brain. In order to achieve her goal of becoming an ace chef, she had to put her personal life on hold.

Well, starting tomorrow, she would make every effort to plan a date with at least one online candidate. What's the worst that could happen? So maybe she'd encounter a few duds along the way. Better than growing into an eccentric old woman who wore too much rouge for her own good.

Jess slammed off the faucet and hopped out of the tub. She slipped on her white terry robe and wrapped it tightly around her. Shivering, she returned to her room, opened the closet door, and pulled out her long, black skirt.

A lot of single women blossomed, even thrived, without a husband or children. But she was not one of those women. She yanked her white silk blouse off the hanger, paused, and studied the evidence in her hand. Why this outfit? Because

Tom said she looked great in it? *Bad idea.*

Jess tossed the blouse on the bed, hastily unzipped her skirt and climbed out of it. She scanned her overflowing closet for a garment that wouldn't scream desperation and settled on her blue cotton dress.

Her craziness had started when she'd seen Tom with Heather in Flavors. If she didn't watch her step, she'd turn into Juan's ex-wife.

Jess slid her dress over her head. Too bad she'd overheard Juan's sad commentary to one of the waiters. He said his ex didn't want him and didn't want anybody else to have him. Perish the thought!

Jess plugged in the blow-dryer, flipped her hair forward, and let the warm air travel over her neck. She couldn't possibly be so petty. Tom deserved a wife who would make him happy. Very happy. But just not Heather. Heather Webster was all wrong for him. So why couldn't he see that? And in telling him, would Tom believe her, or would she only succeed in breaking his heart?

Pulling the dryer away from her hair, she held her breath. The doorbell? She snapped off the noisy device and waited. The sound of the buzzer traveled to her ears like a symphony.

Smiling, Jess dropped the dryer on the bed and dashed to the front door.

❧

Tom adjusted the knot in his tie, then picked up his suit jacket off the bed. He glanced at the phone again. "Nope." As much as he loved Jess, his days of pursuing her with undying patience had come to an end. Love had to be mutual, or it bordered on pitiful. Time to move on.

He strode to the front door and grabbed his car keys off the hook. His hammering heart disagreed with him. No surprise. But the truth had set him free. Free enough to carry on a nice chat in Instant Message last night with Linda—also known as Lab711.

Tom locked the front door, then proceeded down the long, carpeted hallway. Second thoughts made him hesitate at the waiting elevator. But he groaned and stepped inside. If he intended to make a go of it with another woman, he'd have to quit harboring hope for him and Jess. His sixteen-year trek had dragged him over rough terrain—from starry-eyed schoolboy to thirty-two-year-old prisoner of hope.

Tom exited the elevator into the parking garage under his building. No sense feeling guilty. He'd done nothing wrong. If Jess wanted a ride to church, she could've called him or she could ask the doorman to hail her a cab.

Sitting behind the steering wheel of his vehicle, Tom shook his head. One word from Jess that this was her favorite truck, and he'd run out and bought one. *Pathetic.* He'd been so blind he'd let himself believe that, once Jess reached her career goals, her eyes would open to discover romantic possibilities with him.

Tom shifted into drive, headed out from the gloom of the underground garage, and squinted at the bright morning greeting him.

Men had done crazier things in the name of love. How about Samson? Now there was a guy who'd learned a lesson or two on where to set the bar when it came to the opposite sex.

Blowing out a long breath, Tom grimaced. In all fairness to Jess, she was no Delilah. Jess had a good heart. She'd been dealt her share of problems. And allowing herself to fall in love with him would be tantamount, in her mind, to betraying her father.

According to Jess's dad, Dean, he was the only one who could be trusted with his daughter. Tom grinned. Talk about a left-handed compliment if ever he'd heard one. Though he had been a willing victim, not seeing himself as victimized at all, as long as he got to spend time with Jess.

But Jessica Stewart no longer needed tender loving care— at least not the brand he offered. She was a grown woman. A beautiful, successful woman, who didn't require coddling.

Tom pulled the truck into a spot in the church's gravel parking lot. He cut the engine and looked up to see Frank heading toward him. Opening the door of the truck, Tom nodded a greeting.

"Where's Jessica?" Frank leaned sideways to peek into the cab of the truck.

Tom hopped out, closed the door, and pressed the key chain to set the alarm. "Not with me." His sarcastic tone would no doubt give rise to Frank's suspicions.

"A lover's quarrel?" Frank quirked his dark brows. As they headed in the direction of the front entrance, his smile slowly disintegrated.

Tom shook his head. "Sorry, but I can't joke about this yet." He'd never be able to joke about losing Jess.

"Nah. I've got a big mouth. Ignore." Frank clapped his hand to his shoulder. "And here's Jess now," he said between clenched teeth.

Tom's jaw grew taut as Jess breezed toward him. He took in the color of her dress, setting off the clear blue of her eyes. At her tentative smile, he made an effort to recall the pep talk he'd given himself this morning. He approached as the new Tom—no longer a prisoner of hope. "Morning, Jess." He returned her smile as Frank made a hasty retreat up the church steps.

"Hi. What happened to you this morning?"

"You could've called me if you needed a ride, you know."

Her perfectly arched brows rose in what seemed like surprise. "Oh, well, in any case, Marilyn came by to pick me up." Jess glanced over her shoulder. "She went in the side door." She cleared her throat. "You know, to bring the kids to the nursery."

Tom nodded. "That's nice." He ran a quick gaze over her face. His heart had to be oozing admiration all over his sleeve. "But you could've called me if you needed a ride." Hadn't he said that before? He looked down, focusing on the cement steps, but Jess's scent alone was enough to force him down on one knee.

"Well." Jess laughed. "You usually call me. I—I didn't know what was going on with you since. . ."

Tom lifted his gaze to her. "Since?" He tilted his head but couldn't break the code on her unreadable expression. Seized by an insane desire to reach out and touch her, he clamped his hands behind his back.

"You know what I mean. I thought, now that you're seeing Heather—"

Tom laughed. A nervous reaction to her show of jealousy.

Jess shot him a wide-eyed look of indignation. "What's so funny?" Her shoulders straightened in a defensive posture.

"I'm not dating Heather." Tom tugged at the knot in his tie. "I would've thought you knew my type by now."

"Well, that's fine too. I didn't want to come between—" Jess ascended another step. "Some people don't understand that men and women can be friends." She smiled.

Tom's heart made a rapid descent to the sidewalk. He had been one of those people. "That's right. Some people don't." Just the kick in the head he needed to get on with his new life. Could the Lord show him any more clearly?

They walked past the outer doors together, moving through the sanctuary and greeting friends as they headed toward the third row, center aisle. To Jess, this was business as usual. Anything more came from his overactive imagination.

Settling into his seat, Tom slanted her a glance. "I met an interesting woman on the Internet."

"Did you?" Staring straight ahead, Jess nodded slowly. "So you joined the Christian dating service after all?" She turned, facing him fully, her eyes darkening. "The one you told me *not* to join?"

"Yes, but it's different for"—*you*, he was tempted to say—"some women."

"Wh–what?" Jess leaned forward, looking like a rocket ready for blastoff. The middle-aged man sitting to her right gave Tom a shrug that said, "Don't look at me."

"We'd better save this conversation for another time." Tom directed his attention to the elderly redhead standing at the pulpit. She'd been making the announcements every Sunday for the past several years, but her name refused to register in his addled brain.

"Yes, we'll talk later. In fact, why don't we go to Flavors for dessert after the service?"

Jess's tone struck as the calm before the storm. But he could do worse than some alone time with Jess.

six

Jess hefted her purse strap to her shoulder and edged out of the pew behind Tom. If only she hadn't told Marilyn on the ride to church not to wait for her after the service. But she couldn't have anticipated then how much she would need her friend's shoulder now and a hefty dose of her humor.

Following Tom up the aisle, Jess collided smack-dab against his solid back. She blinked, quickly registering that he'd stopped to shake hands with the music minister. "Sorry," she whispered.

Tom glanced over his shoulder and smiled, sending unwelcome flutters to her stomach.

Jess opened her mouth to announce she wouldn't be going to Flavors with him, but the youth leader had diverted his attention.

Somewhere between the praise songs and the preaching, Tom's news had hit full force. He'd met an interesting woman on the Internet. His casual statement, accompanied by a guiltless smile, had echoed in her mind, gnawing a hole in the pit of her stomach even as her Bible lay open on her lap. An innocent bystander would never have guessed Tom had tried to thwart *her* plans. A knot grew in her throat.

But she had to ponder the good. The sermon had forced her to reexamine her motives for wanting to go to Flavors with Tom. She had hoped pleasant chitchat over coffee would prove to him his antics didn't phase her. But her plan looked foolish in the light of the truth of Scripture. After all, in his heart, a man plans his course, but the Lord determines his steps. And He was certainly determining hers at the moment.

As Pastor Rob had read from the book of Colossians, " 'Bear with each other. . .forgive whatever grievances you may have against one another. Forgive as the Lord forgave you,' " her heart made a swift turnaround.

Pretending Tom's offense hadn't cut to the core would accomplish nothing. Unforgiveness had no place in a Christian's life, even though Tom had thrown a fit when she'd brought up online dating. He just hadn't applied the same standards to himself—nor to this *interesting woman*.

Jess felt heat rising to her face. Her lips quivered at the thought of telling Tom she had joined Love Online and she had plans for her own first date. She gripped her purse handle tighter. He'd only think her desperate. Mystery was so much more appealing than the known. Did Internet Woman stir excitement in Tom, while her familiar face forced a yawn?

Scanning the back of his golden-brown head, her gaze dropped to the perfectly tailored suit stretching across his broad shoulders. Internet Woman would probably fall head over heels for Tom's great looks, even before she got a glimpse into his loving heart.

Jess clamped her jaw. The shuffle-stop pace toward the exit set her pulse to thudding in her ears. While Tom exchanged friendly banter, she hid behind the canvas of his dark blue suit jacket, though her shield was the source of the frown pulling at her face.

At the sound of street noises wafting through the open church doors, Jess swept aside her disjointed thoughts. Now was not the time to ramble. She groped for one strong, coherent sentence to articulate the basis for her anger, but her chaotic emotions tangled with random words like so much kite string, cutting off her ability to think straight.

They descended the steps, and Jess found herself standing face-to-face on the sidewalk with him. Shirring up for a confession, she took a deep breath and pinned back her shoulders.

Tom's sugary-brown gaze met hers full force, trapping the air in her lungs. A slight breeze ruffled his thick hair. A hint of his cologne, like freshly sliced limes, washed over her, somehow diluting the strength of her convictions.

Tom rested his strong hands on her shoulders and smiled.

Jess swallowed past the sudden dryness in her throat. Her lips parted, but her tongue stuck to the roof of her mouth.

"Do you want to walk or take the truck?" Tom brushed back the windblown hair tickling her cheek. He tilted his head, his smile fading. "What's wrong, Jess?"

She broke eye contact with him and summoned her voice. "I–I think it's best if I go straight home." Alone in her nest, she could sift through her baffling emotions, uncover the basis for the tears pricking the backs of her eyes. *Not here. Not now.*

Tom ran his hands over her shoulders to her bare upper arms. He pulled her to him, or she went willingly, and he gave her a little shake that merely said, "Old chum."

Jess drew back, but her attempt at indifference left her a limp noodle in his grasp. In her mind's eye, she saw a rogue chef break into her kitchen and spike a perfect recipe with a strange ingredient. Their friendship tasted of something unfamiliar, knocking her senses off-kilter.

Tom grinned. "Come on. Let's talk about it."

Jess's mouth tugged upward in an involuntary smile. She stiffened, only to feel her silly grin growing, reaching her eyes. "I don't know why I'm smiling." Indeed she'd gone from foot-stomping mad to battling some nameless thing flowing between them—all in the space of a minute. Even her wacky sense of humor didn't account for her wild responses to him this morning. She needed to get a grip—and fast.

"It's a nice day." Tom glanced skyward. "Maybe we should walk?"

Jess shrugged—suddenly Miss Wishy-Washy in the flesh— the type of woman Mrs. Gunther warned the high school seniors *not* to become when faced with temptation.

Tom continued gazing down at her, while her noisy thoughts rivaled the congested traffic on Second Avenue.

Jess pulled in a shaky breath. No temptation existed here. Mrs. Gunther tried to keep the girls from falling prey to the wrong types of men. "Predators," she had called them. "Handsome. Charming." She'd usually pause at this juncture. "If you're swept off your feet, you just might find yourselves squarely on your bottoms."

Biting back a grin, Jess met Tom's gaze head on. He definitely possessed the qualities Mrs. Gunther had warned them about, but handsome and charming did not a predator make.

Tom smiled, tripping her pulse and sobering her. She cleared her throat. "I think it's best if we skip coffee and talk right here."

Tom pursed his lips, slipped his hands into his trouser pockets, and shrugged. "Okay, Jess—shoot."

She cleared her throat. "It's just that I never want anything to ruin our friendship, Tom—"

"Neither do I." A line formed between his brows, then quickly disappeared.

"Okay, then—I have to let you know I'm angry with you about the Internet thing." She crossed her arms over her midsection, waiting for logic to slow her racing pulse.

"I see." Tom scrubbed his hand across his jaw. "I noticed a change in you after I mentioned—" He dipped his chin and assessed her with narrowed eyes. "Are you angry because I met a woman online?"

"What?" Jess spat the word. Her nails bit deeper into the flesh of her arms. "Is that what you think? That I'm jealous?"

"I don't know." Tom shrugged. "That's how it looked to me."

The wind kicked up. Jess shoved her hair back from her face. Glimpsing her wild-woman reflection in a store's glass window, she tried to smile, without success. "I'm not upset that you met a woman. *Believe me.* It's how you met her."

Tom glanced over his shoulder. "How was I supposed to meet her? What is acceptable in Jess's dating rules for me?"

Jess cringed inwardly. She was speaking too loud. Closing her eyes, she waited for calm to kick in. Even in the face of cranky, unreasonable customers, she could always depend on her self-control. Yet here she was, a hissing steam kettle ready to blow. "The Internet is fine by me. Remember? But when *I* brought it up, you made me feel. . ." *Idiotic. Desperate.* She tilted her chin. "Why is it a valid option for you?"

Tom ran his gaze over her face slowly. "I see your point."

Jess held her breath. He knew her better than any human rightfully should. Perhaps the question hidden in her heart crept into her eyes, screaming, *Why have you changed?*

"It is a valid option, okay? I don't know who you'll meet online, and I made a promise to your father. I'm not throwing you into the lion's den. Besides, since when are you desperate to meet someone?"

Jess planted a hand on her hip. "I'm free to do as I please, and what you promised my father is not my concern." Tom stepped back, but she continued like a freight train out of control, her chest heaving. "What's good for the goose is good for the gander, and I signed up for Love Online. So, while you're seeing Internet Woman, I'll be seeing Internet Man." Jess pulled in a long breath. "And I hope he's a Ben Affleck look-alike."

"You know, you are stubborn to a fault."

"Yeah? Well, have fun with Internet Woman." Jess bit her quivering lip. *I hope she's Quasimodo in a dress.*

"Do you need a lift home?" Tom asked through clenched teeth.

Jess shook her head and swallowed around the lump of grief in her throat. "See you later." She pivoted and walked forward quickly, forcing buoyancy into her steps.

A truck rumbled past, puffing out black clouds of smoke. If Tom called her name, she couldn't hear above the clamor. But wishful thinking battled against what she knew without turning back.

Jess picked up her pace and knuckled the tear at the corner of her eye. Their perfect friendship had changed. Only for the worse.

❧

"What possessed you to do such a nutty thing? I left one detail up to you and—oh, man. I can't go to Flavors with her." Tom pushed back from his desk. He should've known he'd live to regret introducing Linda's friend to Frank through E-mail. But Linda had been adamant about making their first meeting a double date.

Frank held up his hands in a motion of surrender. "Flavors is our favorite haunt, and Wednesday is Jessica's day off—you said so yourself." He smiled, not winning any points. "I thought we'd impress the girls with—"

"They're *women*, Frank." Tom cupped his hand to the bunched muscles in his neck. "The last thing I want is to run into Jess when I'm with Linda." He shoved back his shirt cuff and glanced at his watch. "I'll send Linda an E-mail. Let her know there's been a change of plans."

"At this late date?" Frank got to his feet. "She'll never see it."

Tom continued glaring at the culprit, his mind racing. "Unless you have a phone number for Linda's friend."

"Brittany?" Frank shook his head. "Nope."

Tom nodded his defeat. "I thought I told you to make dinner plans at Harry's." He stood, gazing out the window blankly at the ominous black sky between buildings. "Be aware—I'm going to pummel you if Jess is working tonight. If she doesn't pummel me first, that is."

"What's up with that anyway?"

Tom twisted toward Frank's annoyed voice. "I don't want to add insult to injury." Jess had every right to be angry. He had practically mocked her when she wanted to join Love Online. And now this.

"What?" Frank shrugged. "You're acting like you're married to Jess or something."

Tom dropped to the edge of his desk and sighed. "It'll make for an uncomfortable situation, that's all."

Folding his arms, Frank quirked his brow. "Another mystery solved."

"Forget it." Tom went around the desk and lifted his suit jacket from the back of the chair. "They're meeting us in front of Flavors, right?" He walked to the door with Frank on his heels, flicked off the lights, and locked up. As they strode through the red-carpeted foyer, resentment burned in him.

"Yeah, why?" Frank finally said, his voice bouncing off the walls in the large, marble-floored reception area. He punched the elevator button, and the doors opened immediately. "Forget to slip off your wedding band?"

Touché. They stepped into the mirrored elevator, and the doors closed with a soft *bing*. As they descended to the lobby, Tom watched a grinning Frank drag his hand through his dark hair, appearing pleased with his ill-conceived plan.

"I guess this is your way of helping me get over Jess?" Tom ground out the words before exiting the elevator.

"That is rich." Frank snorted a laugh and gave him a jab in the arm. "You requested the honor of my presence at this gig."

Tom hesitated, clamped his jaw, and pushed open the glass door. No sense arguing with a guy who just didn't get it. They strode to the curb, waiting in the light drizzle for a taxi. "Even *you* know this is in bad taste."

"Ouch." Holding his hand over his heart, Frank feigned hurt feelings. "Lighten up, will you?" He waved and whistled, bringing a cab to a screeching halt at the corner. "The only way to get through this is to face it head on. Be a man."

They hopped in, and Tom gave the young, bearded cabbie Flavors's upper eastside address. He settled back, expelled a breath, and unbuttoned his suit jacket. He scrubbed his fingers through his damp hair, eyeing Frank. "What if Jess is working tonight?"

"So what if she is?" Frank shook his head. "I'll tell her I was the one who made the plans. Happy?"

Tom turned to the window and fixed his gaze on the wet pavement. He hummed to the music traveling from the radio through the plastic divider, but uninvited thoughts nudged their way to the fore.

When he'd decided to start his new life, he never intended to hurt Jess. He liked order. No diverging paths. Perhaps Jess was right about his mathematical mind, but he had tried to prepare for every eventuality. No surprise twists and turns— like Jess's speech after the service on Sunday. Prepared? With her dark hair wild, her blue eyes flashing, he'd been a half step from pulling her into his arms and pressing his lips to hers.

The cab swerved and skidded to a stop, jolting him out of his daydream. He'd like nothing more than to pick up some Chinese take-out, go back to his apartment, and maybe phone Jess. They'd watch a movie together via phone, chat between commercials—

And he'd be right back where he started. Tom sighed and gave Frank a sidelong glance. "I'll take you up on that. If Jess is working tonight, you tell her you made the reservations." It was time to move on. He had reconciled to the fact that this was ordained.

Frank grunted in the affirmative as the cab turned the corner.

Tom looked past the cloudy divider at Flavors's green awning, flapping a greeting against the wind. Two women stood beneath it, chatting.

"That has to be them." Frank rubbed his hands together like a happy camper.

"Yeah, must be." Tom glanced at the meter, counted out bills for the fare plus a tip, and stashed the money in the metal tray. "We'll get out here," he told the driver.

"Good idea." Frank pulled out some cash. "In this traffic it could take ten minutes to get to the middle of the block."

Tom pushed his hand away. "I've got it." Judging by Frank's demeanor, he was in repenting-for-his-blunder mode. As much as he wanted to cut him some slack, he couldn't help suspecting his friend's motives. "What do you have against Jess?"

"Nothing." Frank laughed. "Except the fact that she makes you pathetic, and I'm sick of watching it." He craned his neck and wiggled his brows. "Hey! From here the ladies are looking mighty fine."

"Right." As they drew closer, Tom's heart flipped at the sight of the willowy brunette. If the fragile blond hadn't been standing beside her, he'd declare the woman was Jess waiting for him to give her a lift. *Jess.* He had to push her out of his thoughts right now.

The women stopped speaking and looked up simultaneously before Tom approached the brunette. "Are you—"

"Linda," she said. Her bluish-green gaze held his, and she returned his smile.

Tom shook her proffered hand, while Frank made small talk with the blond. "And this is Brittany." Linda gestured to her friend.

After they'd met each other, Tom held open the door, then followed the threesome. What kind of twisted logic had compelled Frank to choose Flavors as their meeting place? With a

Jessica clone, no less. He mounted the steps to the hostess station, where the owner's daughter Brea nodded a greeting.

"Table for four," Frank said.

Tom bit back the question burning on the tip of his tongue. *Is Jessica in tonight?* He scanned the tables as far back into the restaurant as he could see. His gaze stopped at the corner booth. The dark head of long hair grabbed his attention first. The man sitting across from her—

"Tom?" Frank's voice broke into his jumbled thoughts.

Forcing his attention away from the man—from Jess— Tom's gaze traveled from Frank, to the hostess, then to Linda, who seemed to be restraining a smile. "What?"

"Our table is ready." Frank indicated with a stern look.

Tom nodded. Following behind the group, he fixed his gaze on the booth—and Jess, chatting with a distinguished-looking character.

Tom pulled out a chair for Linda, then chose a ringside seat for himself—directly opposite Jess's table.

seven

Jess's gaze strayed from Jim Hunt's face to her forkful of salad. Her stomach grumbled as her date continued his rags-to-riches saga. Scarlett O'Hara's story didn't drag on this long.

"I opened my third location in 2001." Jim paused. Not long enough for her to answer, but just enough to make sure she heard every angst-filled memory.

Jess took the cue, nodded interest, and plunked down her fork. If only she could enjoy the getting-to-know-you phase, but she and Jim didn't click. The sad realization hit the minute Jim strode through Flavors's dining room, pumped her hand brusquely, and dropped into the booth with an air of let's-get-down-to-business. Jim was obviously used to getting what he wanted. Jess prayed *she* wasn't it.

Judging by the glances shooting her way, the employees silently concurred. This was not a match made in heaven. But she was on Flavors's safe turf, and the staff knew not to let on that she worked there. If Tom's Internet warnings proved valid, there'd be evidence—witnesses.

Jess bit back a grin. At five-feet-seven, she towered over Jim. Her poor choice to wear heels didn't help the matter, and her self-consciousness over her height troubled her far more than the fear of being accosted.

"This year I'll be opening my fifth office." Jim sat back and crossed his arms as if to say, "There—digest that."

"Wonderful." Jess ran her finger over the itchy hive blooming on her forehead. No need to stress. According to Marilyn, all this would be funny—in retrospect.

"A lot of hard work. I had to put my company first." Jim's

eyes shifted as if he'd given away computer underworld secrets. "And I guess that's how I ended up single at forty-one."

"I see." Perhaps the overhead lights picking up the silver-gray at his temples and the deep grooves in his forehead made him appear older. Or maybe she'd grown accustomed to seeing Tom sitting across from her. His intelligent eyes, usually etched with humor, gave her the perception he was the forever-young man she'd met in high school.

"So? What's your excuse?"

Jess choked on her drink. "I beg your pardon?" Despite her initial misgivings, she'd promised herself to stick with the date until the Lord indicated otherwise. But things were sliding downhill fast.

Jim grabbed a slice of crusty bread from the basket. "Why are you still single?"

He delivered the blunt question with a sarcastic edge. Jess watched him slathering butter on the bread. "I'm single because—"

Dora bounded past their table for the third time. Jess forked salad into her mouth, chewing while scrutinizing the waitress's face. Dora's green eyes widened, then shifted in a clandestine signal that left her clueless.

Frowning, Jess redirected her gaze to Jim and surveyed the crumb-littered table. She had to find a tactful way to end the date before the entrées arrived. And before she exploded like the cork on a bottle. "Same as you, Jim—I put my career first."

He grinned around a mouthful. "But I'm a man. Most women regret putting off marriage and children in favor of a career." He drank water, making a *glunking* sound, his Adam's apple bobbing. "No offense. But Christian women especially. Aren't you searching for the things of God?"

Jess's spine snapped straight, drawing her upright from the hunched position she'd maintained to make herself appear smaller. But clothed-in-self-confidence-Jim certainly didn't need a boost from her. "I may have put marriage on the back burner, but I'm not—"

"Sorry?" Jim's sparse brows curved in a show of skepticism. He smiled and smacked his lips. "Great bread."

Jess noted her clenched fists, eased them open, and inched aside the bowl of wilting lettuce. "I guess I'm not *most women*, because I'm not sorry." Of course at times she feared she'd missed the boat, passed her one, true love on the street without ever knowing it.

"Forget it. I didn't mean to hit a nerve." Jim brushed aside the crumbs, scattering them over the surface of the wooden table.

"You—I—" She picked up her glass of iced tea. If she didn't occupy her mouth, she'd have to repent later for what might tumble out of it. Tipping her head, she knocked back her drink the way John Wayne did before a showdown.

"Hello, Jess."

Cold liquid splashed over her chin and onto her white blouse. She gulped, set down her glass, and stared up at Tom. Clutching the linen napkin, she dabbed her mouth in an effort at composure, fully aware she was gawking.

"Tom." Jess's lips pulled into an easy smile. Her pulse raced. *Tom.* He'd come to rescue her. Later, he'd help her find humor in Jim's obnoxious comments. To hear the joyful rhythm of her heartbeat, anybody would think Tom was her one, true love.

"How are you, Jess?" Tom smiled, but his tone alerted her to something amiss.

"Great—I'm great." She turned toward Jim. How could he not feel the dot of butter shining on his chin? She squelched the urge to reach across the table and spruce him up a bit. "Jim Hunt, this is Tom Winters."

Jim popped out of his chair like a jack-in-the-box. "Nice to meet you."

"Yes, same here." Gazing down, Tom shook his hand. He had to be remembering her insecurity about being taller than men, though Tom's handsome face revealed nothing.

Jess took a sip of tea, waiting for Jim to sit, then chanced another glance at Tom. "So what brings you into Flavors tonight?"

"I'm here with Frank"—Tom gestured with a tilt of his head—"and a couple of friends."

Her heart paused, then sank. But, no, after Sunday's argument, Tom wouldn't squire Internet Woman into Flavors. He wouldn't rub salt into the wound. Holding fast to that belief, Jess peered around him.

She caught sight of the back view of Frank, sitting at a table about twenty feet away. Her gaze moved on to a smiling woman who could've easily passed for her sister.

Jess swallowed past the thick ache in her throat, nodded hello, and found her voice. "Oh, good—I see you snagged table 12. Your favorite."

"Yeah, well, Frank made the reservations, but, um. . ." Tom cleared his throat and glanced over his shoulder. "Anyway, I've got to get back to—"

"Okay, then—see you." Jess stabbed her fork blindly into the salad, nearly knocking over the bowl in her zeal.

"Right—and nice meeting you, Jim." Tom turned away.

Jim's response mingled with the sound of her blood coursing through her ears. She watched Tom walk toward his date. The woman eyed him like a grinning Cheshire. Tom dropped into the chair beside her, leaned next to her ear. An invisible band tightened around Jess's ribs. "That's only Jessica," Tom had to be whispering. "She's just an old friend."

"Er, as I was saying. . ." Jim's voice pulled her attention from the numbing spectacle. She desperately wanted to *shush* him. "Is that your ex or something?"

Jess's hand went to her forehead. She rubbed the hive that

had swelled to a hard, inflamed tumor of anxiety. "No, why do you ask?"

"Because I don't want to be involved in anything messy. We can leave now—go someplace else, whatever."

"No, of course not." Abort the date mid-salad? Skulk past Tom like a pathetic castaway with a spotted face and tea-stained blouse? "I'm fine. I—" The touch of a hand on her shoulder made her jump, mocking her words and garnering a scowl from her date.

"Oops. Didn't mean to scare you." Dora pointed to the bowls. "May I take these?" Her eyes flashed another code-red signal.

"Yes, sure." Jess glanced in the direction of table 12 to indicate her awareness to Dora. Understanding passed between them, and the waitress pressed her lips into a straight line of condolence. "Don't be sorry," Jess wanted scream. How many times would she have to explain to Dora that she and Tom were just friends? After tonight there should be no more questions.

Their entrées arrived quickly, but the laughter drifting from two tables away zapped her appetite. Jess sliced her steak into manageable bites, but the food was tasteless to her. The small talk with Jim, agonizing. And the burden of not looking Tom's way, unbearable.

She had to seize the opportunity now, while Jim was shoving beef Wellington into his mouth. Jess peeked out of the corner of her eye, sucked in a breath, and disguised her shock with a cough. *Impossible!* Thomas Winters, fastening a carnation into Internet Woman's hair, on a first date!

Sixteen years of friendship, and she'd seen only Tom's sweet, shy side. Perhaps it was the only side he'd chosen to reveal to her.

"Excuse me." Jess pulled the napkin off her lap, placed it on the table, and slipped out of the booth.

Jim raised his gaze to her briefly. "Fine, fine."

Jess jetted across the restaurant toward the lavatory, carrying with her the image of her best friend turned Romeo. She pushed through the bathroom door, swung it closed, and jiggled the latch with trembling fingers until it slid into the locked position.

Sagging against the door, Jess closed her eyes and tried to breathe. "What am I doing? Acting crazy." Pushing herself off the door, she moved to the sink and clasped both its sides with her hands for balance. "Lord, please don't let me faint. Please don't let me faint." Slowly she lifted her gaze to the oval mirror.

Jess sucked in a sharp breath at the hideous reflection staring back at her. She brushed her fingers over the fresh crop of red welts trailing down her cheek to the right side of her neck. No wonder Tom had never pinned a flower in *her* hair.

She unzipped her purse in haste. She wasn't acting crazy. She'd lost her father. She couldn't bear to lose her best friend, or whatever would remain of him after Internet Woman was through.

Fishing her notebook from her purse, she ripped out two sheets of paper, then shook her bag until she excavated a pen.

An impatient *rat-a-tat-tat* on the bathroom door made her jump.

"Just a minute," Jess called, scribbling the first note to Jim Hunt.

❧

Smiling on the outside, Tom poured himself another glass of sparkling water. Of all the nights for Jess to be here. He had a hunch she'd seen him help Linda affix a flower to her hair, and he'd actually been tempted to apologize to Jess.

Tom shot another glance across the room. Jim sat alone, eating at an alarming speed. Jess's sudden, mad dash to the ladies' room apparently had no impact on the guy, while his own stomach did somersaults. He had to let it go—let her go.

Tom switched his gaze to Linda. The restaurant lights had been dimmed, and he admitted to himself with some reluctance that she looked radiant by candlelight.

Another part of him—the piece that still felt obliged to protect Jess—prompted him to keep watch for Jess's return from the rest room. Jim must've said or done something to upset her.

"Tom, we're losing you again." Laughing, Frank looked from Brittany to Linda. "You have to forgive Tom. He has a brilliant financial mind, but he's socially challenged."

Brittany giggled. Linda patted his arm. "I think Tom's doing great—socially and otherwise."

Tom offered Linda a smile of appreciation. "Why, thank you. I—" He sobered at the sight of Jess making a hasty retreat toward the exit. His protective instincts raised him out of his chair slightly, and he shifted in an effort to cover his jerky motion. None of his business anymore.

Frank, never one to miss a trick, turned to Brittany, filling the awkward silence with cheery banter, and the two quickly resumed jabbering back and forth.

Tom twisted in his chair toward Linda, opened his mouth, then snapped it shut. Where should he begin? He could start with an apology for not really being here tonight. But that would require further explanation—the truth—which included sixteen years of pining. He could almost hear the scrape of Linda's chair against the wooden floor as she bolted for the nearest exit.

"Do you want to go after her?" Linda spoke softly, but her words stung.

"That obvious, huh?" Tom looked toward Jim's table again. Dora stood there, her hand pressed to her cheek, no doubt apprising him of Jess's disappearance. Dora would try to smooth things over, not unlike his efforts to protect Jess for far longer than he cared to remember.

"Are you in love with—?" Linda asked without inflection.

"*Jessica.* I was." *I am?* The double date seemed more a burden now than a blessing. He craved some private time with Linda, a woman who seemed not to judge him. But baring his soul on a first date would be the epitome of selfishness and more than he cared to share tonight. "You weren't set up. I didn't plan on coming here. We ended up—"

"I know." Linda smiled. "Brittany and Frank made the arrangements."

"Did I hear my name mentioned?" A grinning Frank waved his hand as if he couldn't care less and picked up his chat with Brittany.

Linda placed her hand on his. "Do you want to go for a walk after dinner? Just the two of us?"

Tom shrugged. Even now his heart was dragging him toward the exit, out the door, to comfort Jess. "Frank's right. I'm not very good company lately."

"Let me be the judge of that." Linda's blue-green gaze captured his in an expression that told him she held no animosity. "Brittany has to go home early anyway. How about that walk?"

Tom nodded. "Sounds good." And it did. He caught Dora's attention and signaled for the check. Instead of coming to their table, Dora summoned him with a crook of her finger.

He and Frank split the tab, walked to the door together, and divided into twosomes outside. "Good. It stopped raining." Frank winked before departing with Brittany, their arms looped.

As Linda walked beside him, Tom dipped his hand into the pocket of his suit jacket. The note Dora slipped him was still there. He wadded it up in his hand. He would read Jess's letter—eventually. But now. Now belonged to Linda, and he intended to be the gentleman his father had taught him to be.

Tom cleared his throat. "I'd like to apologize again. I don't make a habit of being rude, but I—"

"No apology necessary. I was in love once."

Linda's hand brushed his, but he made no attempt to hold her hand. He'd been a cad all night.

"By the way"—Linda smiled—"I think Jessica and I look a lot alike."

Tom couldn't help grinning. "Believe me—I noticed." Keeping Jess out of his thoughts when he was with Linda would be an uphill battle.

"Why did you guys break up?" Linda stopped midstep, looked up at him, and grimaced. "Sorry—it's none of my business."

"No, that's all right." They strolled one long city block after the other, mostly in comfortable silence, and ended up sitting at a wrought iron table at an outdoor café on Second Avenue.

Maybe it was the warm May night or sipping cappuccino as a light breeze ruffled her shiny, dark hair, but talking to Linda came easy. He hadn't bared his soul, but he'd answered all her questions honestly. "Do I get an award for world's worst blind date?"

Linda smiled. "I will say"—her smile faded, and she met his gaze—"Jessica's blessed to have a friend like you." She rested her chin on her fist. "May I humbly suggest you tell her you're in love with her?"

"Thanks, but it's too late." Tom nodded his certainty. "If anything, this online dating thing has caused us to drift apart." Besides, he wouldn't mind getting to know Linda Anne Baker better. He'd been so busy filling her in on the gaps in his life, he'd discovered little more than her full name and that she worked as a registered nurse in a hospital somewhere in Manhattan.

Linda glanced at her watch and frowned. "Sorry, but I've got to be on my way. What if we get together again sometime?"

Nodding, Tom smiled. "Sounds like a plan."

They wound up the evening promising to pray for one another, for God's perfect will to prevail in their lives, then took separate cabs home in opposite directions.

Tom stared out the taxi window. He knew less than nothing about Linda's circumstances, but the Lord did. He could only pray generally until they met again. Next time he'd let Linda do all the talking. This dating thing would take some getting used to.

The cabbie pulled in front of his building. Tom reached into his pocket for the fare and remembered Jess's note. He stashed some bills into the metal receptacle.

"Have a great night." The driver gave him a mock salute.

"You too." Tom exited the cab.

Tonight's events proved one thing. He had a long way to go till the sparks of hope for Jess were completely extinguished.

eight

Sitting at the table, Jess gazed unseeing at her open Bible. The sound of the gurgling coffeepot, the aroma of fresh-ground beans filling her kitchen, hinted at an ordinary Thursday morning.

Nothing indicated she had grappled all night to bat away tormenting questions. Drenched in sweat, she'd leaped out of bed twice, paced, prayed, and searched her Bible and her heart.

Why had she written Tom the note?

One haunting truth emerged—the sight of Tom, openly falling for another woman, left her with a lingering sense of dread. The ensuing panic at the initial sight of them together had sent her running from the table in Flavors, then drove her pen across the paper to compose a note, which upon reflection she might have written while in a trance.

Jess pulled in a jerky breath and glanced at the digital clock on the coffeemaker. The minutes rolled around to eight A.M. exactly. She stood, lifted the cordless, and pressed SPEED DIAL. *Please, Marilyn, pick up.*

"Praise the Lord, Keith speaking."

"Keith?" Jess winced. "Sorry to disturb you so early." The background music at the Johnsons' included a crying baby, clanging utensils, and Marilyn warning, "You'd better eat those pancakes!"

"Another crisis, Jessica?" Mercifully, the humor in Keith's voice came through. She could almost see the blond, broad-shouldered minister grinning at the other end of the line. He looked like a beachcomber, but he lived passionately for God.

"Keith." Jess twisted the belt on her robe, mentally paring

her long list of troubles. "I wanted to ask—" A child's high-pitched squeal stopped her cold. "It's not important really. It'll keep till Marilyn has some free time."

A burst of laughter reached her ear. "My honey-bun hasn't had free time since Nathan was born. But not a problem—she's right here."

Jess opened her mouth to protest—

"Morning, Jessica."

Too late. "Marilyn. I shouldn't have called."

"Of course you should have."

Jess combed her fingers through her tangled hair, a rat's nest testifying to the angst-filled hours of darkness. "I–I saw Tom last night."

"Tom? Didn't you go out with—what's his name?"

"*Jim.*" Goose bumps skittered over her arms. She pulled her robe tighter. "Please. Don't remind me."

"That bad?" Marilyn offered a moan of condolence. "Well, if it's any comfort, I've been there."

"Yes, I know." Jess took her large clay mug from the cabinet. "I guess I wasn't prepared for how depressing it would be. Everything was forced. Artificial. You know?" She poured coffee and set down the glass pot. "After last evening I'm truly convinced I'll end up alone." She swaggered to the table, hot liquid splashing over the rim of her cup onto her bare toes. "Do you think the Lord meant for us to meet our mates online?"

"I don't know, Jess. All I can say is, I can't complain." The warmth in her voice conveyed her deep affection for Keith.

Jess smiled. "Your husband is one in a million, Marilyn." She sighed. "But I'm afraid this Internet dating thing isn't for me."

"Come on—you said you'd give it five tries. One down, four to go."

"I know what I said, but that was before Jim." Jess floated

a paper towel to the tile floor, pressed her foot to it, and began mopping up the coffee spill. "You're a lot more adventurous than I am. I risked something new and look what happened. I spent the evening dodging the boasts of a narcissist."

"Nothing awful happened, Jess. This guy may not be a match, but—"

"*Isn't* a match, Marilyn. He definitely is *not*."

"Fine, but there are hundreds of Christian men on Love Online. There must be a few diamonds in the lot. Just a sec, okay?"

The sound of muffled voices told her Marilyn had covered the mouthpiece. Jess closed her eyes. She had to find a way to reclaim her self-respect in Tom's eyes. If only she could turn back time, tear up the note, flush it—

"Hi, I'm back."

Jess grasped the wooden chair for support. "I'm still here."

"Keith said he'd watch the kids so I can shop. Maternity stuff. But would you like to come along?"

"Yes, definitely." Jess slumped into the chair. "I need to talk to you." She massaged the dull ache at her temple. "I did something *very* stupid."

"Um. . .is this the part about Tom?" Marilyn giggled.

Jess's stomach clenched. "I'll tell you when I see you."

༺༻

Sitting in a big armchair in the dressing room, Jess remained a silent observer—except for "oohing" and "aahing" along with the elderly saleswoman as Marilyn modeled maternity gowns.

Marilyn, pregnant with her third child, was hunting for a fancy dress for Corinne's wedding. The invitation from her only remaining single friend had arrived in her mailbox back in February, virtually sucking the breath out of her. Everyone in her group had predicted Corinne, a.k.a. The Brain, would be the last to don a gold band. The feisty redhead had been preoccupied with accumulating one degree or another.

Tilting back her head, Jess closed her eyes. Tom had restored her hope on that particularly cold, gray day. "We still have each other," he'd said, instantly dissolving her panic. But Tom didn't phone last night—or this morning.

"Jess? What do you think?"

Her eyes snapped open to see Marilyn pirouetting in front of the three-way mirror. The satiny blue gown puffed, then settled against her bulging tummy.

Motioning with a thumbs-up, Jess nodded. "It'll do the trick, for sure."

"Okay, then—sold." Smiling, Marilyn disappeared behind the dressing room curtain, the saleswoman at her heels.

Jess instinctively crossed her arm over her own barren womb and steered her thoughts to the words the Lord had dropped into her heart in the wee hours. *Fear not, for I am with you always.*

Her eyes burned. *Let Your presence be all I need for peace and contentment, Lord.* But fear—the opposite of faith—had been her constant companion lately.

Jess sighed. Huffing, puffing, and unzipping noises drifted to her ears. Chances were, she'd never try on maternity clothes. She'd been the dutiful daughter, practically scaling mountains to please Daddy. She'd put on hold her deep-down dream of having a husband and children—a storybook family—so she could make him proud of her career achievements.

Jess held tight to the cushioned chair arms. Guilt sliced through her. Instead of being grateful for all her father had done, she was blaming him for shoveling the pit in which she found herself now—the last single woman in her crew of friends.

The saleslady emerged from behind the heavy, green

curtains, looked down at her, and smiled. "Do you have children?"

Already fighting tears, Jess swallowed past the knot in her throat and read the gold name tag pinned to the woman's navy blue dress. *Thelma*.

"She doesn't have any *yet*." Marilyn's muted voice rallied as if in her defense. "But someday soon."

Thelma pretzeled her thin, wrinkled arms over her mid-section, her blue eyes dancing. "You're certainly young enough. Never had children myself." She sighed. "And at seventy, I'm not expecting one anytime soon." She twittered a laugh.

Jess chewed her bottom lip, eyeing Thelma as she labored over the haphazard pile of clothing. Bending slowly, the frail woman picked up a blouse and slipped it onto a hanger with shaky hands.

Before she knew it, she'd be Thelma. Only she'd be breaking *her* back over a steamy grill in a greasy-spoon diner to support herself.

"I lost my husband about a year ago." Thelma extracted another plastic hanger from the snarled jumble on the metal rod. "Harry."

"I'm so sorry." Jess stood to her feet and grabbed a dress from the mountain. "I'll help. I'm getting bored sitting here."

"Oh, aren't you a dear." Thelma sat on the battered folding chair and continued sorting. "Harry used to take me every-where." Looking off, she smiled as if her paramour stood in the distance. "Silly me—never learned to drive. He'd wait in the beauty parlor a whole *hour* till my hair was done. My sis-ter takes me now." She patted her gray, sprayed hairstyle and sighed. "But she doesn't wait for me."

"I can't drive either, but—" No, she couldn't say she had a friend who'd whisk her away anytime, wait for her with a patient smile. Her heart told her those days were gone forever.

"How long were you married?"

Thelma stopped fastening the snaps on a silky black dress. "Ten years and a month."

Jess pulled her gaze from the woman's gnarled hands. She felt a sweat break out on her brow. "You must've met late in life." She clamped her teeth over her bottom lip. She had no right prying into the woman's business, searching for answers to her own pathetic situation.

"No, no, Harry and I grew up in the same neighborhood. Bensonhurst." Thelma rested her hands in her lap. "If you want to know the truth, I was too *fussy*. Turned him down again and again till he got tired of asking." She stood and heaved a sigh. "Eventually he married. I didn't. I realized too late—Harry was the only one for me. Never did meet anyone like him after that. Oh, well, we all make mistakes."

Mistakes? Pressing her hands to her cheeks, Jess shook her head, mentally rewriting Thelma and Harry's story. "But then you did get together in the end." Her voice rang frantic in her own ears.

"Yes, I heard through the grapevine that Harry's wife had passed away." Thelma lifted her bony shoulders in a shrug. "A little investigating and I found his phone number."

Jess searched for breath. Was this how she would end up? Stalking Tom at seventy after he'd lived a life with another woman? And usually women outlived their husbands. What if she never had the opportunity?

Marilyn suddenly appeared at her side, her dress slung over one arm. "Are you ready?"

Jess nodded. "Nice meeting you, Thelma."

"Same here, Dear. Come back when you're pregnant."

"I—I will." Jess floated toward the register, her heart skipping beats. A doomsday feeling washed over her once, then again.

"I'm so thankful I found something for the wedding."

Marilyn tapped her charge card against the countertop. "Three weeks away and I—"

"Do you think I'm fussy?" Jess licked her dry lips. "Be honest."

"You mean picky? About clothes?"

Tamping down the irritation of talking quickly, Jess shook her head. "No. About men."

"Fussy about men?" Marilyn muttered under her breath. She signed the credit card receipt, snatched the garment bag, and tilted her head. "Which men?"

"Marilyn?" Jess huffed a breath. "You're being evasive."

They rode down the escalator, then walked across the store and out the door in silence. "Don't mind me." Marilyn wore a repentant smile. "You know I like to think before I speak."

"And what do you think?" Jess kept her gaze glued to Marilyn's face as they merged into the lunch crowd on Fifth Avenue. "You can be honest."

"*Fussy* may not be the right word here." Marilyn's thoughtful frown relaxed. "You're very accepting of your friends' choices in men."

"Yes, I love Keith. And, well, you're right." Jess felt a relieved smile tug at her lips. "I can't think of any of my friends' husbands whom I dislike."

"By the way." Marilyn hesitated midstep on the sidewalk. "You mentioned that you saw Tom last night." She pointed to a diner. "Mind if we go in here for a bite?"

Jess nodded, though an upside-down stomach replaced her appetite at the mere mention of Tom's name. Pressing her hand to her purse, she felt for the cell phone. Still there. Still silent.

"Good—we got a table." Marilyn tagged behind the hostess.

Jess gathered her wits and followed. The scene in Flavors flashed in her mind all over again. Unless she imagined it, the smile Tom's date had given her conveyed a mixture of pity and condolence.

Finally seated and looking across at Marilyn, Jess folded her hands on the tabletop. "While I was with Jim in Flavors, Tom showed up with his Love Online date. Can you believe that?"

Marilyn's brows pulled together. "So what?"

Slumping against the chair, Jess stared. "You don't think it's a little conspicuous—just a tad crass? Maybe awkward for him to have brought his date into *my* restaurant?"

"Honestly?" Marilyn snapped the menu closed. "No, I don't, Jess. You said yourself you two are only friends. Maybe he likes the food, *Chef.*"

Jess's shoulders sagged. *Would no one understand?* "He didn't do it on purpose."

Marilyn squinted. "Who didn't do what on purpose?"

"Tom. He stopped by our table to say hello." The memory gave her heart an unwelcome jolt. "I introduced him to Jim, and Tom, standing next to him, looked so—" She shuddered. "I can't handle another flashback. Anyway, Tom happened to mention that Frank made the reservations. Frank was there with a date too."

Marilyn nodded slowly. If she was getting the picture, her blank expression showed no signs of it.

"In any case I couldn't bear another moment in Jim's company, and with Tom there—" Jess slid to the edge of her seat. "I went to the rest room, wrote Jim a note of apology for having to leave, and gave it to Dora to pass on to him."

"You walked out on your date?" Marilyn's mouth hung open in a circle of awe.

"I took care of the bill. I was nervous, okay?" The better part of judgment told her not to go on with the worst of it. "And then I gave Dora a note—to give to Tom." The confession tumbled out of her mouth as if of its own volition.

A mild gasp escaped Marilyn's lips. "Jess! He was on a date!" She shook her head. "What kind of note?"

"In retrospect a pathetic, ugly note. I asked him to call me." Jess unzipped her purse, dug through its contents, and pulled out her cell phone. "And look at the number of unheard messages I have. *Zero.*"

A waitress arrived at the table, rail thin and jumpy, pad and pencil poised. "Ready to order?"

"Burger, well done," Marilyn said, eyes still round.

"A cup of chicken soup, please." Her topsy-turvy stomach pitched in protest.

"An *ugly, pathetic* note?" Marilyn rested her cheek against her fist. "Care to elaborate?"

"Not really, but"—Jess took a sip of iced water and cleared her throat—"it went something like, 'I hope we're still best friends. I love you and—'"

"Whoa! Back up!" Marilyn brushed a bouncy curl from her forehead. "*I love you?*"

Jess tightened her trembling fingers. "Tom knows what I mean."

"Does he?"

Ignoring the sarcasm, she lifted her chin. "I invited him to dinner at my place on Saturday, with a promise to cook all his favorites." Jess's nervous giggle failed to alter her friend's scowl of disapproval. "You don't think Tom took it the wrong way, do you?"

Marilyn fanned herself with a napkin. "Are you sure you want the truth?"

"Keep in mind that I've been leasing my apartment for less than a year. I haven't had a chance to invite him up for dinner." Jess sat ramrod straight. Spoken aloud, her claims sounded ridiculous. "Tom's been *inside* my apartment—when other friends were there." She pulled in a breath. "So what do you think?"

Marilyn shrugged. "That you were afraid to be alone with him?"

"Ha! You know Tom. He's the perfect gentleman." At least when it came to her.

"I don't know." Marilyn sighed. "The first time you see Tom on a real date is the first time you decide to invite him to your place for dinner—alone. He has to think you're making a play." She put her hand to her throat. "Or that you're a jealous maniac. And I'm beginning to think it's the latter."

"*Oh, yuk!*" Jess said as the waitress set down their plates, then shot her a scathing look. "I didn't mean *yuk* about the food." The woman strode off without acknowledgment. "I'm a mess."

Smiling, Marilyn quartered her burger with a knife. "Tom's going to call, Jess. I'm sure of it."

"Right." And even if he did, where would they go from there? "Tom pinned a flower in his date's hair. Can you believe that?"

❧

Tom declined Frank's invitation to lunch. Preferring the solitude of his office, he phoned the deli to have a sandwich brought in and retrieved Jess's wrinkled note from his pocket.

Sitting at his desk, he flattened the paper on the blotter. Last night he'd only scanned her letter. And when his head hit the pillow, he thanked the Lord he hadn't read anything into it.

Before walking out the door to work this morning, he stuffed the note into his pocket for the sole purpose of reexamining his motives before flat out refusing her offer of dinner at her place.

Clasping his hands behind his head, Tom pulled in a deep breath. A man with a big ego might interpret her sudden interest as a sign of jealousy. If jealousy had provoked her reckless, uncharacteristic behavior, he'd have no part in it. But if she sincerely wanted to maintain their friendship, how could he refuse? As a man of his word, he intended to keep his promise to Dean to look out for Jess. He just wished she wouldn't tease him. He had no illusion that Jess's note meant anything other than she didn't like seeing him with another woman. Well, he was no saint there. He hadn't liked seeing her with another man either.

Tom picked up the phone, turned it over in his hand, and shook his head. If Jess needed him, she knew where to find him. He was through with following her like a puppy at the heel, nipping and hoping for any sign of attention. Life went on. And he must, too, or he'd spend his life alone while he watched Jess keep him at bay.

Shuffling through his stack of phone messages, he pulled out the one from Linda and dialed her number.

nine

Jess crushed the sofa pillow to her ear and rolled onto her side. Kiwi's tweets and whistles grew louder.

Chucking the pillow, she sat upright and looked across the living room at the little green merrymaker. Hopping happily from perch to perch, the parakeet appeared innocent of intruding on her nap. Rehashing her idiotic antics over lunch with Marilyn had left Jess too edgy to sleep.

Pushing up from the sofa cushions, Jess strode across the room to the cellular phone on the desk. The phone's glass window told her what she already knew—*no new messages*. She took a deep breath, cleared her throat, and dialed Tom's office. Enough of her childish behavior.

One ring. . .

She pressed the DISCONNECT button and shook her head. Perhaps she should plan what she wanted to say. Pacing in front of Kiwi's cage, she stopped and hit REDIAL. There was no good reason to act like a stuttering schoolgirl with Tom.

One ring. . .

Jess loosened her grip on the phone, lest she pop its plastic innards.

Two rings. . .

"Good afternoon, Mr. Winters's office."

On hearing Fran's familiar voice, Jess's mouth formed words without sound.

"Mr. Winters's office," Fran repeated.

"Oh, Fran, hello, it's Jessica."

"Why, hello, Jessica. I haven't seen you in quite awhile."

If the middle-aged, prim, and proper assistant suspected trouble brewing between Tom and her, she was too professional to let it creep into her tone.

"I've been working hard, you know." Jess ran her tongue over her parched lips. "I was just wondering if Tom's around. But if he's too busy—"

"Tom's in his office. Just a moment. And, please, come visit soon."

"Will do." A jaunty tune replaced Fran's voice. Jess pressed her hand over her thudding heart. *Now what?* She dare not ask him why he hadn't phoned, though he had a nerve.

"Hi, Jess, what's up?"

Tom's curt greeting drew strength from her legs. "Are you busy?"

"I'm expecting a client any minute, but—"

"Sorry." The roots of her hair tingled with embarrassment. She cleared her throat. "I was just wondering if you got my note. . .if Dora gave you—"

"Yes, I got it."

And? Treading the carpet like a terrified mouse, Jess stopped for a breath. "So can you make it on Saturday?"

"Really, I'm sorry, but I can't."

He didn't sound a bit sorry. "Oh, that's too bad." Jess slapped her thigh. She could do without the whiny voice. "I guess you're busy?"

"Yes, I have plans."

"Well, then. . ." Jess resumed pacing. *What kind of plans?* She'd once had the liberty to ask without giving it a second thought. A deep sadness settled over her. But if she didn't follow up with a comment, she'd risk being a bigger fool in Tom's eyes. "So how did your online date work out?"

"Actually, pretty good. In fact, Linda's the reason I can't make it Saturday."

Twisting, Jess caught a glimpse of her stunned reflection in the mirror. "A second date then? Good for you." Her voice broke, betraying her words. Fighting her rising dismay, she pulled in a deep breath. "Can you come for dinner Friday instead? We can catch up on things."

"Don't you work Friday nights?"

"Usually." Her face heated. "But I can trade days with Melanie. You know, the new assistant chef."

"I see." Tom's sigh wafted to her ear, sinking her heart. He wanted a polite way out. But why should she make his departure any easier on him? "I don't know, Jess. I—"

"Well, what is it?" She spat the words, hurt suddenly veering to anger. "Do you have plans with Linda tomorrow as well?" Jess clamped her hand over her mouth. She wasn't a jealous maniac, but she'd done nothing to deserve getting kicked to the curb—for a stranger.

"No, I'm *not* seeing Linda tomorrow night." The edge in Tom's voice made her shudder. She had to learn a whole new way of speaking to him, of tiptoeing around certain topics— Linda being one of them.

Jess pressed her hand to her chest, hoping to still her thudding heart. "Then maybe you can make some time for your friends." She could get through this. She'd not allow anger to destroy what little remained of what they once had. "This friend in particular?"

Another sigh. "All right, Jess."

If she harbored any spark of hope that they'd return to the way they were, the sound of his resignation extinguished it. Anger sifted out of her, leaving grief in its wake.

"Jess? What time should I be there?" Tom's voice was softer now.

"How about six? Is that good for you?" A shiver of humiliation ran up her spine. The self-conscious words passing between them reeked of formality—a prelude to what would eventually dwindle into a final good-bye, she knew.

"Six o'clock sounds—just a sec," Tom said. "My client's here, but six sounds fine. I'll see you then."

"Yes, I'll—" The line went dead.

Jess set down the phone and dropped into the chair beside the oak desk. Smoothing her hand across the cool wood, she looked at the framed photo of her smiling father. "See what happened, Daddy." A sob lodged in her throat. She pressed her lips into a tight line and swallowed. "Even you couldn't plan for this. But it's not your fault."

Jess slipped out of the chair, dropped to her knees, and closed her eyes. "Please, Lord, don't let Tom fall in love with Linda."

Sweat tingled on her forehead. "That's not a valid prayer, is it? If it's not Linda, it'll be another woman. I pray for *Your* perfect will to be done, Lord, not mine. I trust You know what's best for me." Tightening her laced fingers, she rocked forward and pressed her head against her hands. "But what if I've fallen in love with—"

Her throat swelled and ached. Jess scrambled to her feet, knocking the porcelain sailboat to the rug, pushing the unthinkable from her mind. Even in her dreams, the words were too dangerous to utter.

Tom had never shown a romantic interest in her. Jess set the knickknack back on the desk. She had to face facts—she just wasn't Tom's type. And if she threw herself into his arms—even once—her heart would forever be in his hands. Somehow she'd always known that.

Jess strode across the room to the sofa, sat down in front of her laptop, and snapped down the keys to sign on to the Internet. She promised herself four more dates. She couldn't give up on pursuing her dream—not yet.

Scrolling through her E-mail, she clicked open the first with *Love Online* in the subject header.

Dear Loves God (Nice handle),

I'm fairly new to Internet dating, and though I've met an interesting member, your profile captured my curiosity. (For personal reasons, I prefer to date several women until I know where the Lord's leading.)

Jess nodded. "Now that's honest enough."

Like you, I'm in my early thirties and live in midtown Manhattan. It seems our similarities outweigh our differences. If after reading my profile you agree, and you'd like to meet me, please send me an E-mail, and we'll make arrangements.

Best regards,
TCTwo

With trembling hands, Jess hit the REPLY button. "Please, Lord, don't let this be another Jim."

No one could replace Tom, but a couple of dates might help fill the gaping void he'd left in her life. Short of begging, she'd practically had to twist Tom's arm to get him to agree to dinner.

Imagine, trying to persuade him to see her as more than a friend? Jess shook her head and typed, *Dear TCTwo. . . .*

⁂

Frank slammed his fist into his palm. "You're getting suckered right back into it, Pal."

"Thanks for looking out for me, but Jess is a friend." Tom shrugged into his suit jacket. "She's extending an olive branch, and I can't turn her down."

Crossing his arms over his chest, Frank dropped to the edge of the desk. "Don't say I didn't warn you."

"I promise I won't." Striding to the door, Tom hit the light switch and turned. "Planning to sit in my office all night?"

They walked to the elevator in silence. Frank's shadow felt like a weight on his shoulder—a good angel or a bad angel, he couldn't decide. Tom pressed the elevator button and leveled a gaze at him. "You really dislike Jess, don't you?"

Staring down at the floor, Frank shrugged. "There's no denying she's drop-dead gorgeous, but she's driving you crazy."

The words were a punch to his gut. Suspicion hit, turning his insides cold and tightening every muscle in his body. "What? Is it a love-hate thing? Are you interested?"

Frank's laugh echoed through the reception area. "Yeah, like I have shot with that. . .*princess*."

Tom's pulse kicked up. He jammed his foot against the elevator door to hold it open. "What's that supposed to mean?"

"It means nothing, huh?" Frank slapped him on the shoulder. "Calm down."

"I am calm." Clenching his fists, he pulled in a breath. "What if you did have a shot with Jess? Would you take it?"

Brushing past him, Frank stepped into the elevator.

Tom followed, hit the LOBBY button, and slanted him a glance. He'd been confiding in Frank for the past five years. "Forget it. Doesn't matter one way or the other."

Frank ran his hand down his tie and grinned. "I should learn to mind my own business."

"Yeah, you should."

They both laughed. But Frank hadn't given him a straight answer.

Parting company with a handshake, he watched Frank head across the avenue, dodging traffic against the light. There went a guy who loved taking risks. And he loved winning even more.

Tom hailed a taxi. He could still cancel. If he had a drop of good sense, he'd go straight home.

Staring at the bearded cabbie in a turban, he gathered a breath and ground out Jess's address.

A heap of regrets swelled his heart. Only one woman could cause him to lose it—and he was heading toward her apartment right now.

Loosening the knot in his tie, Tom slumped against the seat. Acting solely on unfounded suspicion, he'd gone off the deep end, turning FBI agent on Frank, grilling the guy as if he stood between Jess and him.

Strumming his fingers on his knee, Tom stared out the side window. If Frank did make a play for Jess, she'd never go along with it.

But what if she did? Tom shook his head. He'd be forced to grin and bear it. Better still, he could accept the transfer to California.

Tom watched workers streaming out of the office buildings on Fifth Avenue as the blare of car horns assaulted his ears. A change of scenery might do him some good. *Out of sight, out of mind.* Maybe. . .

But then there was the other, more dangerous, adage. *Absence makes the heart grow fonder.*

Tom strode down the long, carpeted hallway toward Jess's door. He could've found his way blindfolded to the heavenly scent of brisket. In the scheme of things, this night would mean a great meal and a few laughs. Nothing more.

The door opened. Jess's clear blue gaze locked on his, her smile, her orange-vanilla scent, crashed over him. His thinking mind disengaged. Squaring his shoulders, he fought to recall his convictions.

"I'm so glad you could make it."

Her voice was melting chocolate on his tongue. He uttered something unintelligible and followed her into her apartment. "Thanks for inviting me." After she closed the door, he handed her the bouquet he'd bought, with much reservation, in the shop beside her building. His visit wasn't meant to give any false impressions—not even to himself. "They're not roses, but—"

"Thank you." Jess pointed to the sofa. "Have a seat while I put these in water. And dinner will be served in"—she glanced at her watch—"precisely five minutes."

As he drank in the warmth of her nearness, he made no motion to move. "Sounds good."

Jess smiled again. "I've missed you." She placed the flowers on the coffee table behind her. With one step, she closed the gap between them and wrapped her arms around his waist.

Tensing his arms at his sides, Tom clenched his fists. She couldn't do this to him anymore.

Jess rested her head against his chest. Tom closed his eyes, allowing himself to inhale the flowery scent of her hair, even while his mind commanded him to stop.

Snapping to sanity, Tom stepped back, out of her embrace, lest he bunch her in his arms and never let go. The hurt glittering in her eyes tempted him to apologize. He tried to smile, change the subject. Blind to his attraction, she'd think he'd rejected her as a friend. "I—"

Jess twisted away and headed toward the kitchen. "I'd better check on the brisket."

With his senses spinning, he made his way to the sofa and sat down. *Pride cometh before the fall.* Guaranteed, he'd never attempt a feat like this again. Another second of her in his arms and—

And what? Tom stood, raked his fingers through his hair, and scanned the photos on the mantel. "Food smells great, Jess."

Only the sounds of clanging pots and pans traveled from the kitchen. Tom closed his eyes. He hadn't meant to hurt her. He'd never hurt her intentionally. He'd always returned her hugs, but—

"I made the broccoli and cheese wraps you order in Flavors."

"Great." His gaze traveled around the room. She'd made some changes since his last visit, but the Raggedy Ann and

Andy dolls he'd given her still sat side by side on the wooden chest, making his heart clench. She cherished their friendship, and he'd just trampled it. "The place looks great."

The pine dining room table, set for two with candles and linen, would've once sparked hope in him. But he'd do well to keep in mind that seeing him with Linda had provoked Jess into action. Nothing more. Jess needed to test—to find out if she still held first place in his life.

Tom returned to the sofa. If he could hold fast to truth tonight, he'd not allow the distraction of her nearness to rule his passions.

"So." Jess appeared in the doorway, untying the white apron at her tiny waist. "Are you ready?"

No. Tom stood. "To the table?"

"Right here." She pulled out a spindle-backed chair.

Tom met her gaze, hesitated, and smiled. "Thanks—for all of this."

"That's what friends are for."

True. And *friends* was all they'd ever be.

ten

Jess buzzed around the kitchen, out of Tom's view, gathering cups and dishes for the dessert phase of their meal. Her hands shook as she poured fresh coffee from the glass pot into two mugs.

She was barely able to speak through dinner, though she should have been grateful Tom had shunned her innocent hug. Imagine if she'd been her chatty self—not rendered sullen and heartbroken by Tom's rebuff? She might have offered him her heart right then and there.

Jess placed the coffee mugs beside the two plates of apple pie. Her pulse pounded harder, her face heated. She *wouldn't* cry. By God's grace she wouldn't cry. The sooner Tom left her apartment, the better.

He'd either catch her stealing covert glimpses of his taut, muscular forearms, or he'd see right through the thin shell of her cool veneer to the overwhelming misery beneath the surface—the realization that she'd never be in his safe embrace or nestled against his strong chest.

Biting her quivering lip, Jess scooped vanilla ice cream onto the slices of pie. What if this was their last time together and Tom died away to a dim memory—jammed into the already stuffed closet in her head? Thoughts of him would emerge, slip under the door, same as they had with her dad tonight.

"A woman should never chase a man, Jess. Remember that. Nothing will make a guy run faster." If only she had recalled her father's words of wisdom *before* coercing Tom into dinner. Now she looked like the desperado she was. It would be

one thing if it was just some guy—any guy. But Tom? Oh, how it mortified her.

Tom's reserved demeanor told her he wanted to beat a path out her door, even while he ate, stopping to give her polite compliments. He had already started a new life. And if she didn't get on with hers, she'd be left in the dust, wallowing in self-pity.

Jess drew a deep breath. Right now she had to summon enough composure to navigate the living room with the tray laden with hot items—and not stumble and scald herself. She would smile her way through dessert. Wasn't she practiced at smiling on the outside? And when it came time to say good-bye, she'd keep her chin up.

Jess gripped the serving tray with both hands. Perhaps they'd get around to discussing Love Online. Now there was a prickly topic guaranteed to burst her balloon—suck the air out of her romantic dreams and plummet her back to earth in a crash landing. She put one foot in front of the other with purpose and entered the living room. "Here we go."

"Can I help?" Tom started to rise from the sofa.

"No, I'm fine," she said, setting down the tray on the coffee table. "I hope the pie's not overcooked or—"

"It looks beautiful, Jess. Smells great." Tom rubbed his hands together, smiled, and pointed. "May I?"

"Please, have at it." Jess edged her way around the coffee table and sank to the cushion beside him. Their arms brushed, giving her heart an unwelcome jolt. A blanket of sadness fell on her as she watched him from the corner of her eye. Her attraction to him had ruined everything. "Is it good?"

"Mmm." Chewing and nodding, Tom smiled. "The best." He picked up his mug, sipped coffee, then turned his cinnamon gaze on her. "Mind if I ask you a nosy question?"

Jess buried her anticipation under a smile. "Sure, shoot."

"What made you walk out on Jim?"

Feeling thumped over the head by the unexpected inquiry, Jess licked her lips, cleared her throat, and swallowed. "Oh, that." Looking away from his magnetic gaze, she grabbed her plate and jabbed the ice cream with her spoon. "We didn't hit it off really." She chanced another glance at him.

Tom's brows pulled together. *"You didn't hit it off?* And that was the only reason you bolted for the door?"

She should've guessed Tom knew her too well to swallow the half-truth. Even Marilyn had weighed her with a critical squint, exactly as Tom did now, as if questioning her sanity.

"I suppose it was a combination of things." Jess studied the melting ice cream while her heart skipped beats. "Jim kept dropping food all over the place"—a*nd you kept laughing with Linda*—"grating my nerves until every crumb could've been a boulder."

"Sorry." Tom snorted a mild chuckle. "Sorry things didn't work out for you, Jess."

His sentiments sounded sincere. Her neck and face heated, but she pushed a smile to her face. "Who knows? Maybe I'll hear fireworks with the next guy."

Resting his elbows on his knees, hands clasped, Tom nodded. "You're going to try again then?"

"Sure, why not?" Jess held her breath, willing him to make an objection. None came. "We can't all be as fortunate as you were the first time around."

"True." Tom scrubbed his hand across his jaw. Thinking. Always thinking. "But even though Linda and I got on really well"—he raked his gaze over her face slowly—"I'm not going to be exclusive this time."

"This time?" Jess burst into laughter, nearly knocking the dish off her lap. "Tom? When have we ever been exclusive? *Whom* did we have to be exclusive with?"

Scraping the last bit of pie off his plate, Tom forked it into his mouth. The dark cloud settling over his features caused her laughter to die on her lips. He set his plate on the table, gently, as if not to disturb the solemn moment—the funeral of their friendship.

Jess sat up straighter, her back as tense as the growing silence between them. Any second now, the black cloud tumbling toward her would hit with full impact.

"Well." Tom cleared his throat. "It's getting late."

Her heart smashed against her ribs. "You know what's funny. I just met a guy on Love Online who mentioned something similar. He wants to play the field. Well, not really—he wants to find the woman God has for him. And I thought it was so honest of him to say that up front. And, well, I wrote back." Jess broke for a breath, though the blaze of Tom's eyes was enough to cut short her babbling.

"Are you using your real name?"

Perhaps it was her imagination or wishful thinking, but the casualness in his voice sounded deliberate. Her insides perked at his sudden show of interest. "Oh, no, too dangerous." His gaze stayed riveted to her face. She definitely had his full attention now. "Do you want to guess what my handle is?"

A slow smile graced his handsome face. "It has to have something to do with food, right?"

The expectation in his eyes tempted her to nod yes, to reassure him he had won the game. Jess felt a genuine smile warm her face. "One wrong guess. You get two more."

Tom tugged at the knot on his already loosened tie. "Then it has to have something to do with cooking—being a chef?" The urgency in his voice suggested impatience.

Jess bit her lip and shook her head regretfully. "Nope."

Tom cupped his hand to the back of his neck. As much as he loved winning, the look of determination on his face betrayed an underlying frustration that went far beyond their little game. "Okay, Jess, I give up."

"Oh, no, so soon?" Her smile faded. A pang of loss accompanied the certainty that everything had changed between them. "It—it's 'Loves God.'"

Tom nodded slowly. "'Loves God,'" he whispered. "That's nice, Jess. Sweet."

"Thanks." Sipping her coffee, she studied his profile with her lids lowered. The tremor in the pit of her stomach kept her from asking for his Love Online handle.

He glanced at his watch again. "Well, I don't want to overstay my welcome." Tom stood and stretched. The knot in her stomach tightened as she watched him move to the chair where his suit jacket lay and then scoop it up.

Jess sprang off the sofa cushion. "Can I get you more pie? Coffee?" It couldn't be over. Not yet. She needed more time. A little more time.

Patting his flat stomach, Tom shook his head. "No, thanks. Everything was delicious, but I overdid it."

Jess put her hand on his arm. *Please don't go.* "Wait—"

Tom glanced down, then lifted his serious gaze to her face. The red light was on again. She quickly withdrew her hand. "Let me wrap the leftovers for you."

Without waiting for his response, Jess pivoted, flew to the kitchen, eyes burning, heart pounding.

&

Tom stood in front of the mantel, hands in his pockets. He'd done it again. There were hundreds of women to choose from on Love Online. Hundreds.

Was this the Lord's intervention? His handiwork? Like when he wanted to follow his first instincts, refuse Jess's invitation to come here tonight, and in a split second, with his mind saying no, the Lord had prompted a yes.

And that idiotic comment he'd made about not being exclusive. How had he let that slip? Jess thought the remark hilarious. And it was.

"Almost done," she called from the kitchen.

"Sure, no problem." Planted in front of the mantel, he refused to move. He had lingered in the doorway of the kitchen for awhile, watching Jess pack food for him, until a wild urge to hold her, to kiss her, forced him to make an abrupt about-face. He had no intentions of venturing back to the scene of the crime.

"So where are you going with Linda tomorrow?" Her cheery voice drifted into the living room.

Tom's mouth twisted into a cynical grin. Her casual tone indicated she was over the jealousy phase—the catalyst that had prompted her to invite him to dinner in the first place. "Oh, I don't know. Linda likes Italian food. Maybe that place downtown."

Who was he kidding? He wouldn't take her to La Luna. Too many memories of times spent there with Jess. One thing for sure, he needed to make a clean break, a fresh start. "Or maybe the new place on Seventh Avenue."

He eyed the photo on the mantel of a smiling Dean, locked in a hug with Jess. Tom swallowed around the lump forming in his throat. *My job here is finished. Finished. And I promise I did my best.* "That food about ready?"

"Right here."

Startled, Tom turned, crashing into Jess and catching her by the arms. "Sorry. I didn't know you were behind me." They stood within a breath of a kiss. He pried open his fingers, releasing his grasp on her.

"It—it's all right." Jess didn't move.

Desire was back, gnawing at him. Tom inched away and took the plastic bag from her outstretched hand. "What have you got in here? The kitchen sink?"

Jess fluffed her hair and cleared her throat. Her slender hands twisted together. She looked as eager for him to leave as he was desperate for their time together to end. "There's enough food in there to keep you—" She backed up. Not far enough. Never far enough to obliterate his attraction to her. "To keep you fed for a week."

Tom held up the plastic sack. "Well, thanks a lot for this—for everything, Jess." He was crazy to have come here. He strode to the front door and turned. "I guess I'd better—"

"I meant to say before—I'm not going to be exclusive either." Her lips curved in a small smile that didn't quite reach her striking eyes.

"Well, good." Tom put his hand on the doorknob. He was sure Dean was still watching him—only this time from a photo. "Just be careful, Jess."

"I will." Hands clasped behind her back, chin raised, her smile slipped.

A stab of guilt hit him—a gut reluctance to leave her alone. Tom cleared his throat. "Could I have a glass of water?"

"Oh, sure." Jess turned and headed for the kitchen. "Must be all that salty food."

Tom released his white-knuckled grip on the knob. Jess shouldn't be alone. She shouldn't have to look for a husband on the Internet. He had to shoulder at least half the blame for her situation. If he hadn't been a fixture at her side, she would've had more offers.

He wouldn't e-mail her again on Love Online. He didn't need to drag Jess, or himself, back into a relationship heading nowhere. Still, he itched to burst into his apartment, flick on the laptop, and read the E-mail Jess had sent him in error.

"Here you go." Jess held out the glass, ice cubes *clinking*, assessing him with her cool, blue eyes.

Tom took the tall glass from her. "Thanks a lot." The last thing he needed was to meander, catch another whiff of her orange-vanilla scent. In two long swallows, he drained the glass and handed it back to her.

"See you, Tom." Jess raised her hand in a farewell gesture.

"Yeah." He jerked open the door. "See you, and thanks again."

"You're welcome."

He heard the door close behind him and the finality of the snapping locks as he made his way toward the elevator.

Dragging his fingers through his hair, he looked up and sucked in a breath. *Did You put me in this situation tonight, Lord, or did my weak will bring me to Jess's door?*

As the elevator sank to the lobby, Tom caught a glimpse of his distorted reflection in the metal doors. He looked as if he'd been through a war—a battle all too familiar—flesh against spirit.

In the lobby he slowed his pace and looked around, vowing not to return. His armor had sustained more dents and scratches tonight than he cared to admit. E-mailing Jess, even under a secret identity, would be too dangerous.

He returned the doorman's nod and walked up the street. A light drizzle cooled the air. Tom shuddered and picked up his pace as if he might outrun the sense of desolation closing in on him.

eleven

Jess scanned the coffee table littered with cups and dishes. An hour must have passed since Tom had left her apartment, though she hadn't moved off the sofa or kept track of time. She pulled in a breath and began stacking the aftermath of dessert.

Reliving Tom's rejection would do her no good. If she didn't snap out of it, she'd fall into a useless state—crawl inside herself as she had when her father died. As much as she loved the familiar, loved Tom, the time had come to venture out, let go of the past.

Jess stood and carried the tray into the kitchen. What if Tom hadn't been by her side through the worst tragedy of her life? Her gaze drifted to the calendar on the refrigerator. In a few days she'd have to face the one-year anniversary of her father's death—alone.

Standing at the sink, Jess turned the hot water handle and squirted dish liquid into the pan. She grabbed the copper brush, scrubbed the crusted pot, and shook her head. A tear tumbled down her cheek, splashing into the soapy dishwater.

"What an ordeal." Even Jim Hunt had shown her more warmth than Tom had tonight. Anyone watching from the outside might have thought her a temptress who'd lured Tom into her apartment. Well, maybe she had. Trickles of guilt washed down her back. Hadn't that been her true motive? To get Tom to act the way he used to? To tell her in his special way how beautiful and delightful she was? She swallowed hard. Those days were over now.

Jess pitched the brush into the pan, turned off the faucet,

and dried her hands. She pressed the dishcloth to her damp face, tossed it on the counter, and returned to the living room. She would have to learn to carry on without Tom. He'd go on and get married, and they wouldn't be friends then anyway. This was for the best. Better to have it over now, before she had to watch him fall in love with another woman.

"It's time to eat, Kiwi." Jess shook the box of seed beside his cage. Edging along his perch in anticipation, the parakeet studied her with black beady eyes. "Tom was awful tonight, Kiwi. But I suppose I deserved it." She filled his dish and hooked it inside the cage. "We probably won't be seeing him again."

Swallowing past the knot in her throat, she meandered to the window and pressed her head against the cool pane. "I admit it, Lord. I feel lonely and alone." She knew the Scriptures—the Lord's precious promises. He'd never leave her nor forsake her. And, before looking outwardly for peace and joy, she'd have to grasp, deep down, that she was complete in God.

But when Tom walked out tonight, she felt a piece of herself die. Maybe their friendship had been founded on an unhealthy dependence upon one another. Never the way God intended for a man and a woman. Without the benefit of marriage, where had they been heading anyway? She didn't know. But the path they'd been traveling together suddenly diverged, leaving her alone to venture into unknown territory.

Turning from the window, Jess sighed and scanned the quiet room. She would practice godliness with contentment, look upward, not outward, for joy the world couldn't give and had no power to take from her.

Her gaze lingered on the laptop on her desk. The machine seemed to beckon to her. Jess approached the desk slowly and circled the chair once before yielding to the temptation to sign on to the Internet. How pathetic was she? Actually looking forward to an E-mail from a complete stranger? But that stranger was the only hope she felt at the moment. The only glimmer that maybe she wouldn't spend her life alone. Oh, he wouldn't be the one, most likely, but if he could find interest in her, someone else would as well. Just not Tom.

While waiting for the connection, she sent up a silent prayer. If TCTwo had sent a reply, she might make a new Christian friend. Not that anybody could replace Tom. But oddly TCTwo's first E-mail had brought her a measure of peace.

Jess scrolled through her messages quickly, stopping when she saw his E-mail, stuck between the other Love Online responses.

Dear Loves God,
Thank you for responding to my E-mail right away.
Sounds as though you've been through some tough times.

Jess looked at the upper left hand corner of the screen. He'd posted the response at 1:20 A.M. She glanced at her watch. He'd sent it only ten minutes ago. Maybe the Lord had led her to check her mail.

Would it be easier for you if we got to know each other
through E-mail for awhile, before proceeding with a face-
to-face meeting? I've run the gamut myself. Maybe we both
could use some downtime.

Yes, that's precisely what she needed. Downtime. Time to clear the cobwebs out of her head. Time to learn to live on her own. Be her own person. Fly solo. Her breaths came faster.

Do you want to tell me more about this "friend" who let

you down? Personal experience tells me men and women
can't be friends for long, without the romance thing getting
in the way.

"The romance thing." Jess nodded. She would've denied it
up and down a few short weeks ago. She'd scoffed at that kind
of cynicism—*men and women can't be friends*. She and Tom
were living proof those people were all wrong. But, of course,
that was past tense.

Would you like to talk in Instant Message sometime?

Jess bit her lip. She wouldn't decide tonight. She left it a
maybe in her mind and continued reading.

This is probably of little or no interest to you, but there's a
chance I'll be moving to the West Coast in the near future,
unless the Lord directs otherwise. The transfer would be a
good career move, but, more importantly, I'm hoping to
put distance between myself and a certain disappointing
relationship.

Jess covered her mouth with her hand. "Poor guy." She
could certainly relate.

I look forward to hearing from you again soon.

> *Best regards,*
> *TCTwo (Just call me TC)*

&

Tom sat at the kitchen table, staring at the laptop screen,
shaking his head. Against his better judgment, he'd replied to
Jess's E-mail last night.

He'd felt sorry for her, and before he could think straight, he found himself typing—commiserating with Jess as if she bore no responsibility for the gaping hole in his heart.

Pulling in a breath, Tom opened her E-mail message, with the certain knowledge that this charade could spell suicide for their friendship. Whatever was left of it anyway. He wanted to get Jess over the emotional hurdles, without causing her to hate him for the rest of his life when she discovered the truth.

Still, he had prayed long and hard after leaving Jess's apartment, and he'd gotten off his knees with one strong conviction—if she saw his heart, without attaching his friendly face to it, the truth might finally register.

Dear TC,

I like your idea. I'm fine with meeting strictly in E-mail for now. I'm sorry you've 'run the gamut.' And though you seem reluctant to discuss your problematic relationship in depth, I'm afraid the anonymity of this process may bring out the worst in me; meaning, I'm apt to spill too many details if we communicate for a time.

The long and short of it is that my "friend"—I THOUGHT he was a friend—up and dumped me for no good reason. We spent almost all our free time together for the past sixteen years. (Best friends since high school.) And POOF—now he's gone— practically. Perhaps you're right to want to bury your past, move to California, move on. I don't know what good will come of rehashing it all anyway.

By the way, it's fine that you're dating other Love Online members while we communicate. I'll be doing the same. My first date didn't work out well, but I promised myself four more tries before throwing in the towel. After that, I don't know what. But I'm striving for "godliness with contentment."

I hope you write back soon. I feel better already having

shared my woes with a nameless, faceless friend. Say a prayer
for me, will you?

Sincerely,
Loves God—but you can call me "Jess"

"Wow, Jess." Tom snapped down the REPLY button. "A
friend who up and dumped you, huh?" He shook his head
and commenced typing.

Dear Jess,
   It was good hearing from you again. But I'm sorry to hear
about the "friend" who up and dumped you after sixteen
years of friendship.
   Since you weren't romantically involved, how does a
friend "dump" a friend? Is that the same as dumping a girl-
friend? Do you have any idea why he's keeping his distance
from you?
   Godliness with contentment is something we should
ALL strive for. But as long as we put the Lord first in our
lives, He wants to give us the desires of our heart. That
includes marriage and children, if that's what you want.
So keep the faith!
   By the way, don't worry about using me as a sounding board.
Since we intend to date others and we're not romantically
involved, perhaps we can counsel one another? I promise I'll be
praying for you—for us. I trust the Lord will work it out for
the good.

Sincerely,
TC

જ

"Frank's here? Alone?" Frowning at Dora, Jess dried her hands
on her apron. "It's too late to order."

Dora shrugged. "He knows that, but he's here to see you."

Juan snorted a laugh and shook his head.

"What's so funny?" Jess watched the two exchange glances. "If you think Frank's here to deliver a message from Tom, you can think again. After last night's dinner, I have no illusions that Tom wants anything more to do with me."

Still grinning, Juan waved his hand. "Remember when you said men are strange? Maybe they're stranger than you think."

On a sigh, Jess walked past them and into the dining room. Her gaze immediately went to Frank, sitting alone, but looking every bit his handsome, confident self.

Their gazes met, and Frank got to his feet. "Jess, I didn't mean to disturb you at closing time. I'm sure you want to get home, but I—"

"Not a problem." A small tremor started in the pit of her stomach. This had to be about Tom. Frank wouldn't come here on a friendly, I-was-just-in-the-neighborhood visit. His bright smile usually dimmed when she came within ten feet of him. "So what brings you here?"

"Can we sit for a minute?" Frank fiddled with the knot in his tie.

Jess tried to smile. "Sure, we can sit." His demeanor told her whatever business he had would either send her through the roof or sinking to the floor. *Help me through this, Lord.*

Frank's smile disappeared, and his dark gaze latched onto hers. "I'll get right to the point, Jess."

Her stomach flip-flopped, but she nodded slowly.

"One Christian to another, I have to confess I never liked you very much."

Jess drew a sharp breath. She never doubted Frank harbored animosity toward her, but hearing him say it aloud gave her a sickening jolt. "I don't know what I've done to make you—"

"Nothing. Honestly." Frank leaned across the table, his nose nearly making contact with hers. "I judged you, and I had no right."

Leaning back in her chair, Jess studied him, her mind still reeling. "Judged me for what, Frank?"

He pushed his fingers through his black hair, looked around the room, and met her gaze head on. "Tom."

Jess swallowed the rising dread in her chest. The mention of Tom's name caused a tide of panic to float to the surface. Fear and love and loss and hope mingled to suck the strength from her. She opened her mouth to speak.

"Please, let me finish." Frank covered her hand with his.

Everything in her wanted to pull away, but she didn't flinch. Frank had come here, heart in hand, seeking forgiveness. The Lord would expect her to respond with His lovingkindness.

"Tom's my closest friend." Frank looked at her as if in search of a nod or word of confirmation. Jess sat frozen. "Tom even got me my job at Martin Financial." He squeezed her hand and cleared his throat. "Again I realize I was wrong, but I thought you were—a burden to him."

Jess withdrew her hand. "Wh–why? We were friends. We helped each other. I didn't just take from Tom."

"And Tom never said you did. You have to understand it was me, all me. In my boorish way, I thought I was protecting him." Frank shook his head, his dark gaze thawing the icy barrier she tried to erect to protect herself. "If you can forgive me, Jess, I want to turn things around. I'm letting you know I'm here for you—anytime."

"That's good of you, Frank, but—" She shrugged. It was one thing for her to forgive him—and she did. But turning to him as a trusted friend?

"I wouldn't blame you if you never wanted to set eyes on me again." Frank stood and clapped his hands at his sides. "But at least I thought I'd offer."

Jess stood to her feet and managed a smile. "It was brave of you to come here. And I do forgive you, Frank." She couldn't claim she had never judged. "In fact I've been there. Sometimes I see Tom with a woman and decide she's all wrong for him." She looked up into his dark eyes, which seemed to fill with understanding. "I judge too."

Frank's lips spread into a slow smile. "A hug?"

Jess laughed and stepped into his open arms. She heard footsteps behind her, felt Frank's grip loosen.

"Who knew I'd find my two best friends here?"

Turning swiftly toward Tom's voice, Jess's eyes widened as she stared at him mute.

twelve

Jess sat in front of her laptop, grinding her toes into the plush carpet. Writing a stranger an E-mail at one in the morning with details of her personal life bordered on wacky. But she was past caring. And this stranger didn't know her from Adam, so it was safe to vent. She set her fingers to the keyboard and followed her impulse.

Dear TC,

    The worst thing I could've imagined actually happened to me tonight. You know the friend who practically abandoned me? Well, he showed up where I work. (I may as well tell you, his name is Tom.)

    Our mutual church friend (Frank), who's also Tom's coworker, had stopped by to talk with me. Talk, and that's all. Frank apologized for holding a grudge against me, asked my forgiveness, then said he'd like to be my friend.

    And in walks Tom. Mind you, this was closing time. I got the distinct impression Tom thought something strange was going on between Frank and me. (We were hugging at the time, but it was all totally innocent.)

    Don't ask me why Tom had come into my restaurant to begin with. (I'm a chef, by the way.) Maybe he wanted to apologize for his "mood" Friday night when he had dinner at my place. (Yet another long story.) But the look on Tom's face scared me. Honestly I thought he might deck Frank then and there— though I have no illusions jealousy had anything to do with Tom's reaction. I'm guessing Tom felt Frank was taking sides— going against him for me. You know, the male bonding thing?

Tom said, "I just stopped by to say hello, but I can see you're busy." At which point I nearly fainted dead away. Even the mild implication that something sinister was going on between Frank and me made me freeze with panic.

I can't understand it, but Frank said nothing to shed light on the situation. In fact, Frank didn't utter a word! And my own mind was so muddled that I don't think I eked out more than "hello."

What do you think? Give me some insight into that male psyche. I'll help you when the time comes in the future.

You said you didn't mind if I used you as a "sounding board"; otherwise I wouldn't have written you about any of this. I figure with E-mail, you can always delete me. In person you might not have such an option. So do you have an opinion? I'm all ears. Keep praying for me, please!

Best regards,
Jess

P.S. I haven't answered your previous E-mail, but more details to follow.

"There." Jess pressed SEND, sat back, and sighed. Men understood other men. TC would give her his unbiased take on things, because he didn't have a stake in her personal life.

Jess snapped off her laptop. Someday she might actually meet TC in person, but for now a face-to-face encounter would only complicate matters. Hiding behind a computer screen certainly had its merits. She could empty out her heart to TC, as she'd once done with Tom—only minus the fear of falling in love.

She dimmed the living room lights and padded to her bedroom. Tomorrow was a new day. She refused to stay up half the night worrying about church in the morning—

pondering how to avoid both Tom and Frank.

Jess sank to the edge of her bed. She'd seen a side of Tom tonight she'd never known. Standing tall and straight, his well-muscled body straining against the fabric of his black shirt, his dark eyes glimmered as if in challenge to Frank.

Her mouth pulled into a smile. Most likely Tom and Frank's friendship would stand the test of time. She only wanted Tom to fall in love with her, not challenge Frank to a duel.

"Wishful thinking." Jess shook her head. There were no duels going on for her heart. But Frank should've explained why he'd come into Flavors, instead of standing his ground, wearing a sinister grin. It was almost as if he wanted to give Tom the wrong impression.

Jess got to her feet and wrestled out of her blouse. All this conjecture was madness. She twisted in front of the full-length mirror and groaned. "I look like a bag of bones." She had two weeks to put on the pounds, fill in the gown she'd wear for Corinne's wedding.

Tom would be there. Maybe something magical would happen. Or maybe he'd show up with a date. Either way she couldn't be looking the skeleton she did. Tiramisu would be her companion at night for the next two weeks.

❧

Tom slammed his apartment door and strode down the hall to the elevator. Friends? Heat spread through his chest at the thought of having to face the two of them in church this morning. I'll give him friends! Putting his arms around my Jess. Frank could be peculiar at times, but he had always respected that Jess was off limits.

Tom tugged at his tie before entering the elevator. Both of them were free agents. He'd only gone into Flavors to try to patch up their friendship. How was he supposed to know he'd find Jess and Frank practically smooching? His stomach roiled at the thought. It was one thing to have Jess out of his life, but in his life and dating Frank? That was not going to happen.

Rubbing his tired eyes, he stepped out of the elevator and kicked aside the soda can in his path. No wonder Frank couldn't give him a straight answer the other day.

Tom marched up the ramp in the musty, underground garage. Every muscle in his body reminded him of his sleepless night—time wasted recalling things Frank had said or done in the past, then weighing them against the scene in Flavors.

And Frank, striding up to him in the gym, comparing biceps. None of his antics had been done in jest. All along he'd been competing for Jess. All their chats in his office and Frank's feigned innocence. . .

Turning the key in the ignition, Tom snorted a humorless laugh. He'd taken long enough to figure out what "I'm just worried about you, Buddy" really meant. But figure it out he did. Frank had been goading him for years to give up on Jess, for one reason only. So that he could make his move.

Well, all the best to both of them. He had a great time with Linda last night. He needed to think about his future now, not his past. And if he could get his head on straight, Linda might be a part of his future.

Still, how could Frank have done this to him? In Jess's case, he could forgive and forget. She'd always been blind to his feelings for her. But Frank—

Tom tightened his grip on the steering wheel. A good thing he knew better than to check his E-mail when he got home last night. An excited message from Jess, telling him all about her new prospect, would've sent him through the roof.

Tilting his head from side to side, the bones in his tense neck cracked. Maybe Jess and Frank deserved each other. After all, the two of them lived in La-La Land—passing up true love while they waited for true love. And here he'd thought Brittany was a perfect match for Frank.

"Hey, Buddy, you want to move it?"

As the rough voice filtered through Tom's open truck window, he jerked out of his daydream and back to chaotic, New York City reality. He glanced into the rearview mirror and felt his ears burn at the line of cars behind him waiting to move forward in midmorning traffic. He was going to have to snap out of the lovesick puppy syndrome.

He drove the two blocks to the church, swerved into the parking lot, and cut the engine. What if Frank had the audacity to drive Jess to church this morning? Tom scanned the area for Frank's car, grunted, and abandoned his search.

If Jess and Frank were openly dating, he didn't want to see it. The two of them arm-in-arm would definitely sell him on the idea of taking the transfer to California. How could he stand looking at a guy who won Jess's heart with a couple of smooth lines, when he'd been laboring for her love for years?

Tom stepped out of the truck and tucked in his tie. He kept his gaze trained on the sidewalk and sent up a silent prayer. The last thing he needed was to bump into Frank and Jess.

He'd somehow found the strength to turn and hightail it out of Flavors last night, but if he saw them lovey-dovey in church this morning, his self-control might fly right out the stained-glass windows.

෯

Sitting in the second to last pew in back of the church, Jess watched Tom make his way down the aisle to the row they usually occupied together. She closed her eyes. One quick look at him brought on a flood tide of unwelcome emotions.

Her rapid heartbeat accompanied the heat of a blush to her face. Anybody with eyes might know she'd fallen head over heels in love.

If only Frank hadn't come into Flavors last night, she would've known Tom's reason for showing up. What if things between Tom and Linda had gone all wrong? And Tom had stopped by to chat and resume their friendship? But if Tom misinterpreted the scene he'd walked in on in Flavors, she'd most likely lost any chance with him.

Jess flipped the pages of her Bible. What Tom did or didn't think shouldn't matter to her anymore. The big picture was what counted. And his cold-shoulder treatment Friday night should've cleared up any open questions in her mind.

"Psst, Jess."

She blinked to the present and turned to see Frank leaning past the elderly couple sitting beside her. "Any room for me?"

Jess shook her head and shrugged.

"I'll move down one," the woman to her right chimed in cheerfully.

Great! "Thank you," Jess said, pulling in her feet so Frank could squeeze past her. Her gaze went to the front, zeroing in on the back of Tom's head and causing her stomach to dip.

Frank dropped into the seat and sighed. "I'm glad we had that talk last night."

"Yes, me too." Jess tore her gaze from Tom. "I don't know if we should—" She cleared her throat. "Never mind." So they were sitting together in church. If somebody wanted to make more of it—namely Tom—what could she do? Tell Frank to get away from her?

Frank tilted his head, brushing his hair against her ear. "I meant what I said last night. I'd like it if we could be friends."

Jess nodded and licked her lips. "Sure we can—why not?" The stupid words tumbled out of her mouth with haste. She didn't want to have to prove them.

"Good. How about a cup of coffee after service?"

No! "Um, let me think. . . ." Looking straight ahead, she caught a glimpse of Tom's profile as he chatted with the usher standing beside him. If Tom turned, even slightly, he'd see her and Frank, and then what?

"Are you okay with that?" Frank said. "Or are you worried about what Tom would think?"

Turning to Frank, Jess frowned. If only he could read the confusion on her face, perhaps he'd let her off the hook. But he smiled, patiently awaiting her answer. Jess cleared her throat. "Why? Do *you* think Tom would be upset?"

Frank gave her one of his nonchalant shrugs. "He shouldn't be. I don't know exactly where you two stand anymore, but—"

"We don't run each other's lives." Jess smiled to take the edge off her retort. "I didn't mean it that way exactly. We're still friends, of course." She clutched her Bible tighter.

"Well, then, good. That's a date." Frank grinned.

As the music started, Jess was left with her mouth hanging open. She stood with the rest of the congregation. She couldn't politely get out of their date now. Is that what Frank had called it? A date?

She gave him a sidelong glance. With his eyes closed, hands lifted, Frank appeared wholly into praising God. Just as she *should* be. And he definitely looked innocent of malice.

Jess closed her eyes and caught up with the lyrics. As she sang each line and note, the here and now drifted out of her mind. Sinking deeper into the presence of God, peace washed over her. Nothing bad would come of any of this. For now, nothing and no one had the power to rattle her world.

❧

Tom sat with his back rigid. Right now he would gladly exchange his pain for the anger he thought he'd feel at seeing Frank and Jess together again.

Struggling to keep his mind on the sermon, he gazed up at Pastor Rob.

"The Lord works out all things for the good to those who love Him." The minister smiled. "We look at our circumstances and sometimes find that truth difficult to believe. But we know every word in the Good Book was written under the inspiration of the Holy Spirit. Tested and tried, every word is true."

Father, forgive me. Tom shifted in his seat. *If it's Your will that Frank and Jess end up together*—a tight knot lodged in his throat—*then I trust You to work it out for the good.*

Neither Frank nor Jess had noticed when he'd accidentally caught sight of them. After the service he would slip out of church by way of the side door. Make it easier on them—and himself.

And if time and distance didn't heal his wounds, if he couldn't forget Jess, he had the option of remaining single. But he had come to one conclusion. In his present state of mind, he couldn't see Linda again. It wouldn't be fair to drag her into the emotional fray.

Shuffling noises from the congregation filtered to his ears, waking him from his revelry. Tom stood, closed his eyes, and repeated the words to the closing prayer. A notion entered his mind, growing in intensity, compelling him to exit the church by the back doors.

His shoulders stiffened in rebellion. The side door would be the easy way out. Tom turned and grabbed his Bible off the seat. He lifted his gaze to the spot where he'd last seen them. No need to take an alternate route. Jess and Frank were already gone.

thirteen

Tom tossed his jacket on the bed, whipped off his tie, and flung it onto the dresser. If he hadn't seen Jess with his own eyes, getting into Frank's car, he wouldn't have believed it. But he had seen them.

A simple misunderstanding, he told himself. It had to be.

Drifting into the kitchen, Tom opened the refrigerator, grabbed the tray of cold cuts, and slammed it onto the counter. Jess had acted pretty casual, calling out his name in the parking lot, then giving him a happy wave before riding off into the sunset with Frank. Why spare his feelings at all?

Tom slapped a few slices of ham onto the rye bread. If he'd had a minute alone with Frank, he would've asked him outright where he planned to take this. But as it stood, his phone messages to Frank's cell and home had gone unanswered.

Overnight, the guy had gone from never speaking more than ten words at one sitting with Jess to Mr. Congeniality. And Frank's sudden interest occurred only since he hadn't been seeing much of Jess. Either Frank saw an opening and used it to his advantage, or all of this was mere coincidence.

Tom bit into the sandwich, stopped chewing, and looked across the kitchen at the laptop on the table. Curiosity may have killed the cat, but he had to know if Jess had emailed him.

He put down his sandwich, sat at the table, and signed onto the Internet. She'd be doing him a big favor if she admitted she had feelings for Frank. At least he could face the brutal truth head on and deal with it.

His pulse kicked up when her E-mail appeared on the screen. "The Lord will work all of it out for the good." He had to believe that. Barely breathing, he scanned her message quickly, then reread from the top.

"Well, what do you know?" Tom cupped his hand to his rigid neck. Frank wanted to be her friend. With all the females walking the face of the earth and Frank's former disdain for Jess, he just happened to want to be her friend. And, of course, according to Jess, Frank's hug was *innocent*.

Tom shook his head. Jess never could read men. She wanted his view? Okay, he'd give it to her.

Dear Jess,

I read your E-mail twice, and I'm of the opinion that this guy Frank shouldn't be hitting on you if he's any friend of Tom's. I know what you said about its being all innocent, but I'm sure Frank is aware that you and Tom have hit the skids, so to speak, and so he's trying to make his move.

Tom read what he'd written and groaned. No, he couldn't manipulate her. If his heart was in the right place, he'd only offer his help. His honest opinion. He held down the delete button and started again.

Dear Jess,

I think you ought to give Tom a call, unless, of course, you have a romantic interest in Frank. Maybe you've got Tom figured all wrong. You stated that he might have come into your restaurant to apologize for acting crummy toward you the previous evening. Do you know what caused this change in him? Is this Tom's modus operandi? *Probably not, since you wouldn't have stayed friends with such a clod for sixteen years.*

What would Tom do if you phoned him? Hang up? What's the worst that could happen? You should give him a chance at least to explain, unless you want to write off the friendship completely.

Have you ever considered that Tom might be in love with you? Why else would he have gotten so steaming mad when he caught you and Frank hugging it up after hours? In fact, that's my conclusion. Tom is in love with you.

I don't know if I've been much help, but I'm trying to be. Oddly enough, while I think I'm helping you, you're helping me. Typing out my thoughts—as opposed to letting them float freely in my mind—has definitely had a cathartic effect. Hope to hear from you soon.

> *Best regards,*
> *TC*

Tom pressed the REPLY button before he could change his mind, delete again, or add a rotten postscript about Frank.

He returned to the counter, looked at his sandwich, and tossed it in the trash. Frank knew how much he loved Jess. How could he have the heart to do this to him?

⁂

Quick and painless, Jess mused, as she exited Frank's car in front of her building. "Thanks for everything."

"For nothing." Frank winked. "I owe you for having read you all wrong."

Standing at the car door, Jess smiled. "You're a good guy, Frank."

Gesturing with a thumbs-up, he laughed. "Just don't let Tom hear you say that."

Jess shook her head, closed the door, and waved. Frank had known Tom for a long time, but he didn't know the real Tom. The Tom who'd never get upset if she called Frank a good guy.

Walking through the lobby, Jess felt her smile fading. She'd made a point of waving to Tom in the church parking lot, only to let him know she wasn't trying to hide anything. But he looked too busy to care anyway. A quick nod and a half-smile and Tom was off.

As the elevator took her to the tenth floor, her thoughts turned to TC and what advice he might have for her. She walked toward her front door, key in hand. After reading her ramblings, the poor guy must've thought she was nutty, and he hit the DELETE button. She probably would have.

Jess tossed her purse on the sofa and made a beeline to her desk. She may as well check for the improbable. She typed in her password, ignoring the ringing phone, as she waited for the machine to pick up.

"Hello, Jess? Jess? You know who this is, and I want the scoop."

She stood, sprinted to the phone, and grabbed it. "Marilyn? Why are you whispering?"

"Because Keith doesn't like me gossiping. But I have to know—what gives with you and Frank?"

"Not a thing." Jess looked heavenward and sighed. "But I had a hunch some people might misconstrue."

"Yeah, some people might, but what did Tom say?"

Jess's stomach clenched in a silly schoolgirl response. "I saw Tom for half a second in the parking lot, just before I left with Frank. But why should Tom—"

"Tom saw you leaving with Frank? You left with Frank?"

Jess hiked the phone off her throbbing ear, into her hair. "Now you're talking too loud."

"Sorry. It comes from raising Nathan. Hold on a sec." A couple of beats later, the crackle of a sigh reached her ear. "I have to go. Keith overheard me yapping, and he says I'm—"

"Gossiping?" Jess laughed. "I suppose Keith thinks talking is gossiping. But don't worry—you haven't missed a thing. And if anything earth-shattering should happen, you'll be the first to know."

After their good-byes, Jess returned to her computer, still chuckling. If only her life were as exciting as Marilyn imagined.

She scrolled up and down through her mail, stopped, and smiled. TC had written back after all. She opened his E-mail. There were only a few paragraphs, but better than no response. As she skimmed his message, Jess gasped. This guy should write soap operas.

Resting her chin on her fist, disappointment traveled to her toes. All she'd wanted was some sage advice, not a script for a fantasy. "Right. I just might call Tom because he might be madly in love with me."

Jess exhaled a deep breath. TC had made one good point. What was the worst that could happen if she called Tom? Of course, Tom wouldn't slam down the phone—because when he heard her voice on the machine, he wouldn't pick up to begin with.

Turning in her chair, she reread TC's E-mail. He had taken the time to write. She at least owed him a response.

Dear TC,

Thank you for trying to help. And I think I'll take your advice and call Tom, at least for friendship's sake.

I'd like to clarify one thing. My last E-mail to you was written in haste, and perhaps I led you to draw some wrong conclusions. (I don't have a copy of the E-mail I sent you, because I delete a lot to prevent overload. Tom calls my computer the "prehistoric laptop." We both believe it was the first laptop ever made.) In any case there's no chance Tom's in love with me. Women sense that kind of thing. Besides, Tom's now seeing someone he really likes. And I'm trying to be happy for him.

Next, Frank and I were not exactly "hugging it up after hours." Our embrace was all about forgiveness. It's too personal to share details, but Frank revealed his heart to me, which I felt was very brave of him.

I'm glad to know this is not a one-way street—that our communication is somehow helpful to you too. I haven't much

*to report today, except that I had lunch with Frank. He's a
great guy after all. But to address your other comment, there
are no romantic sparks between us.*

*I hope to hear from you again soon. If you have any ques-
tions about the better half (females), please ask away, and I'll
help if I can.*

Sincerely,
Jess

After sending the E-mail, she read a few other Love Online
responses, but none piqued her interest. She would open one
more, then haul her carcass downstairs with four loads of
laundry.

An Instant Message popped up on her screen. Jess's hand
immediately went to her thudding heart. Tom?

"Hey, there! What's new?"

Jess's spine stiffened as she typed. "Not much. Nice service
this morning, wasn't it?"

"The parts I heard, yes. I was kind of distracted."

She was thankful they weren't face-to-face. Her heart
pounded so hard that surely he'd hear it. Could he mean—?
She set her trembling fingers to the keyboard. "Distracted?
Why?" The cursor blinked like a clock, ticking off seconds to
a time-bomb.

"I've had a lot on my mind lately. You name it, and it's
probably floating around in my mind."

Where had she heard that expression before? Jess sat up
straighter. "Business problems or what?" She ached to add,
Or did you hate seeing me with Frank? She commanded herself
to stop dreaming. TC had planted the crazy notion in her
head, and now she was running with it.

"Business is business. Keeps me engaged, but I'm glad I
have Frank to pick up some of the slack. You know Frank,
always there when I need him."

Jess felt the blood drain from her face. Did he mean the comment sarcastically? If so, what did she do with it? *Think, Jess—think.* "Yes, Frank and I had lunch after church, and he mentioned what a great team you two make." She held her breath.

"Yep, a great team. Don't know where I'd be without Frank. How was lunch, by the way?"

Jess's breathing returned to somewhat normal. Tom hadn't meant any sarcasm at all. She'd allowed TC's comments to color her thinking. "Lunch was great." Jess deleted "great" and replaced it with "good." Tapping her foot to the tune of her frayed nerves, she licked her dry lips.

"What are you doing later? For dinner, I mean?"

Jess stared at the screen, fingers frozen. This had never been a loaded question in the past, and it wasn't one now. A simple answer would suffice. "I have no plans." Yuk! Why did she write that? Her middle name should be *Desperado*.

"I'm in the mood for Italian. Thinking of hitting La Luna tonight."

Okay, so what did that mean? Was that an invitation? "Sounds like a great idea." Jess heard the *thwack* of the ball as it landed solidly back in Tom's court.

"Want me to pick you up around five?"

Losing her bravado, Jess bit her lip. His invitation shouldn't send whirly-twirlies to her stomach. Oh, but it did. And how could she stop them now? "Hmm, sounds like a plan." She stopped herself from adding that the "hmm" was meant for La Luna's food and not the delicious warmth of his nearness.

❧

Jess sat in the lobby of her building, dressed in her black skirt and white blouse, making every effort to strike a relaxed pose. Any minute now Tom would appear in the lobby, and she would have to act normal. Practicing composure, she stopped wiggling her foot and straightened her shoulders.

She heard the slam of a car door. Her stomach jumped. Though she could see Tom through the glass doors, she knew she was out of sight from his vantage point. Her gaze traveled over him, head to toe, as her nails pressed harder into her palms.

His thick, golden-brown hair—brushed back from his tanned, handsome face—set off his dark eyes. And his broad shoulders. . . .

Jess dropped her gaze to the purse on her lap, studiously avoiding him, until she could no longer ignore the echo of his footsteps drawing nearer.

"Jess."

The velvet warmth of his voice sent the heat of a blush to her face. She stood quickly, sending her purse crashing to the floor.

Stooping simultaneously to fetch it, their heads bumped. "I'm sorry." Jess forced a laugh. The perfect beginning to their evening together.

Tom laughed, handed her the purse, and rubbed his brow. "Anybody ever tell you you have a hard head?"

His humor broke the tension. They walked to the truck together, smiling and exchanging brief glances. But she needed to pull herself together, or she'd be a klutz all night. And Tom, knowing her so well, would see right through her casual façade to the panic beneath.

Tom held open the door and offered his hand to give her a lift into the truck.

Jess placed her hand in his and positioned her foot on the running board. In a blind flash, she was in Tom's strong arms, her cheek pressed against his solid chest.

Jess stiffened. All she needed was to appear too eager. This could be the perfunctory hug of a remorseful friend—

But suddenly Tom crushed her to him, shattering her

doubts, making her senses spin. She melted against his chest, buried her face in the crux of his neck, inhaling his clean lime scent.

Tom drew back slightly, his brown-sugar gaze running over her face slow as molasses. "I've missed you." He leaned down and brushed a gentle kiss to her cheek.

Jess held back a teasing comment that would turn the intimate exchange into a casual moment between friends. She tightened her fingers around his muscular forearms and smiled up at him.

Tonight she would tell him, despite her father's warnings of the perils of women pursuing men. A simple truth from a stranger in E-mail had resonated with her—TC was right. What's the worst that could happen?

Time was running out. She had to know now, or she'd become the lady in the maternity shop, full of regrets. Tom had always been the love of her life. And she had been too blind to see it. The shock of nearly losing him had brought her to her senses. If she kept her love a secret, locked away in her heart, she'd lose him anyway.

Only the Lord knew how Tom would respond. And only the Lord knew how crushed she would be if Tom rejected her.

fourteen

For the past ten minutes, silence filled the truck as they headed downtown. Tom glanced at the traffic light. He strummed his fingers on the steering wheel, slid his gaze to Jess, and smiled.

Tilting her head, she seemed to question his perusal. The dark, silky curtain of her hair fell forward over one shoulder. A jab of longing hit him, exploding in his chest. What did Frank say? *"Drop-dead gorgeous?"* That she was.

He pulled his gaze from her. Even so, Jess's true beauty came from within, radiating from her clear, blue eyes, piercing his heart. It was what had captured him from the second he'd seen her—and each time thereafter. Jess would always be the North Star among ordinary stars. And when he believed his feelings for her had settled, drifted away to a soft whisper, one look at her stirred them all over again.

Tom scanned the heavy traffic ahead. Jess's E-mail to TC made it perfectly clear she was blind to his love.

"You look far away tonight." Jess's voice filtered into his thoughts, and for the first time, he knew she couldn't see through to his bare soul.

Tom tapped the leather seat separating them. "Then come sit closer to me."

Jess's musical laughter rippled over him. Tom smiled. What made him think he could ever get over her? She shifted and draped her arm across the back of the seat. "That's not what I meant, and you know it. So what were you thinking about?"

"Not what. Whom." He slammed on the truck's brakes to make way for a cabbie who sliced in front of him, then glanced her way again.

"Whom?" Jess moved to her former rigid position, slender hands clasped on her lap. "All right then—whom were you thinking about?"

"You, Jess." He had nothing to lose anymore. "I was thinking about you." The tense line between her pretty arched brows disappeared. Her smile said she liked him putting her first in his life, in his thoughts. But he was about to let her down.

"It—it's a green light." Her stressed voice accompanied the tune of honking motorists.

"Green light." Tom accelerated and merged into traffic. He might get his mind on the road instead of drifting on the cloud of her orange-vanilla scent. He would pay the price later, he knew. But another sleepless night seemed a mere pittance compared to not seeing her at all. He had counted the cost before asking her out. And what little time remained until he left New York, he wanted to spend with Jess, even on a friendship basis. "Tomorrow is—"

"A year since Daddy's gone."

Tom shot her a sidelong glance. Her lower lip quivered, and her eyes filled. Poor Jess. Of course the thought wouldn't be far from her mind. He swallowed past the thickness in his throat. "I know, Jess. I—"

"How do you think I'm doing, Tom?" She lowered her lids, twisting her slender fingers. "If my father could see me now, do you think—"

"He'd be proud of you, Jess. I mean that." His eyes burned, and a dull ache wrapped its fingers around his heart. "I'm sorry. Sorry you"—Tom's jaw tightened—"sorry we lost him."

Maybe Dean was the glue that had kept them together. Jess loved pleasing her father. And seeing them together had pleased Dean. She had two men who had loved and protected her, but soon she'd have none.

Jess sniffled and dashed away a tear at the corner of her eye. "We'll see him again in heaven someday."

"Yes, thanks to Jesus, we will." Tom cleared his throat. He had to make their last few times together count for something. How could he leave without knowing for sure Jess could go it alone? "And just watch your father blame *me* if anything went wrong with you."

Jess gave a choked laugh. "Yeah, that would be just like Daddy. So you'd better not skip too many days in a row without seeing me." Her gaze latched onto his, and his heart turned over. "No telling what kind of trouble I'll get myself into when you're not around."

"You'll do great with or without me." The skepticism written on her face mirrored his own doubts. Soon the days between them would stretch into months. Perhaps years. "Tissues." Tom cleared his throat and pointed to the glove compartment.

"Thanks." Jess snapped it open and pulled out the box. She dabbed her eyes and nose. "I don't know what I would've done without you." She pulled in an uneven breath, and he forced away the impulse to hold her, comfort her. "You know, when Daddy died. The Lord and you were my strength."

Tom covered her hand with his, pressing slightly. "You have your church family too, Jess—don't forget that. A lot of people love you." *I love you.* He tried to smile. "Especially Marilyn."

"Yes." She fanned her beautiful face with her hand. "You, and Marilyn, and my other church friends. You're all my family now."

Tom swallowed hard. If he hadn't let his emotions get away from him, he could stay in New York, be with Jess until she met—the man of her dreams. As always, a sense of dread accompanied the thought. "You'll be all right, Jess." Like it or not, he'd been cast in the role of protector. But she wouldn't flounder without him. The Lord was her real protector.

Spotting a parking space, Tom slowed the truck to a crawl. "We'll have to walk about two blocks." He maneuvered the big, black vehicle in reverse. "But I'd better grab this spot." He pushed the gearshift into park, cut the engine, and jiggled the keys.

Jess made no motion to move. She lifted her gaze to him and smiled. "Did I tell you Marilyn's pregnant again?"

He looked past her smile to the glint of longing in her eyes. She'd be happy for Marilyn, but her mind must've leapt to her own ticking biological clock when she'd heard the news. All the more reason he had to get out of the picture, give Jess space to grow and a chance to meet the man God intended for her. *Too bad, Jess—too bad it isn't me.* "So number three's on the way?"

Jess nodded, and what remained of her tears deepened the sparkle in her blue eyes. "Tom. . ." She held his gaze until he thought he might kiss her then and there. "I have something to tell you."

He felt his shoulders tense. The air around him crackled with unspoken emotion. She was about to say something he didn't want to hear. Her lips parted as if to speak, and a dull foreboding told him to run. Reaching in back of himself, he clutched the door handle.

Jess drew in a long breath. "I wanted to tell you—"

"Want to tell me while we walk?" As he studied her serious expression, his breath felt trapped in his lungs.

She tipped her head and smiled. "Good idea. Let's eat first."

They strode toward the restaurant at a leisurely pace, and Jess looped her arm through his. Why couldn't he feel this way with Linda at his side? Sweet as Linda was, his heart belonged to Jess.

But tonight he'd have to tell Jess he'd made a decision to relocate. He was through hiding behind TC in E-mail, and he was ashamed of his reaction when he'd seen her with Frank. Most of all, he was sick of chasing down rainbows.

For far too long, he loved being Jess's hero. But the longer he kept her emotionally dependent on him, the harder it would be on her, and him, when it came time for him to go.

※

Jess clinked her glass of sparkling water to Tom's upheld glass. "Here's to us."

Tom offered what seemed a halfhearted smile. "To us then."

She scanned the cozy, crowded room, with its pale green walls. They had dined here so many times, but this night would be different—either the best of times or the worst of times.

Jess bit back a grin. Tom had held her closer than ever tonight, kissed her as if he meant it. His gesture might've been a sign from the Lord, giving her the go-ahead. Even though Tom had always thought of her as a good buddy, he surely felt the same electricity she had when she was in his arms.

The waiter arrived with their entrees. Gazing down at the steamy plate of pasta, Jess licked her lips. "Looks yummy, doesn't it?" She glanced up, glimpsed his sad smile, and her stomach pitched. "What? What's wrong?"

"Nothing. Looks yummy." Picking up his fork, he swirled it into the linguini. His action seemed more a diversionary tactic than his gusto for food. "I love linguini with clam sauce." He glanced up from his plate. "But yours is still the best."

"Oh, please, nobody's beats La Luna's. But thanks for the compliment." Jess reached into the basket, broke off a slice of crusty Italian bread from the warm loaf, and laughed.

Tom tipped his head, his eyes dancing with the familiar humor she so loved. "I was just thinking about Jim. . .and the bread. He was such a messy eater. If things had worked out between us, I would've had to follow him around with a container of cleaning wipes all the time."

Laughing, Tom shook his head. "Did Jim scare you off? Or have you made another Love Online date yet?" His broad shoulders lifted in a shrug. "I mean, you really should, Jess. Get your ninety-nine dollars worth at least."

Feeling her smile disappear, she forked pasta into her mouth. She'd actually intended to tell Tom she'd fallen in love with him. For crying out loud, he was practically pressuring her into dating other men. "Well, I met one really nice guy, but we'll see where it goes."

"Mmm." Tom swallowed his food and took a sip of water. "Why didn't you make a date?"

Her pulse throbbed harder in her neck, and her face heated. She wanted to strangle TC, but first she would let him know his advice stank. "We want to get to know each other in E-mail a bit longer. We're sort of counseling each other."

Tom fell silent. His handsome face suddenly lost any trace of animation. He gave every indication of being disappointed. He couldn't get rid of her fast enough. This dinner was a sweet gesture of sympathy, but she'd been a burden tonight, crying in the car, reminiscing about her father.

Jess sipped water while she struggled to recover. She had made too much of Tom's kiss. And if she hadn't been so lonely and vulnerable, she wouldn't have magnified the meaning of being in his arms.

She wanted his love so desperately that she'd wished it into being true. "So how about you?" Toying with the food on her plate, she chanced another glance at him. "Getting on well with Linda?" The catch in her voice made her face warm.

Tom loosened the knot in his tie. "Same as you—it's a wait and see thing." He set down his fork gently. Jess tilted her chin, preparing for another blow. "I got to thinking this morning. . . ." Tom stared off for a moment. "In fact, during the service it hit me that staying single is always a viable option."

A cold knot gelled in her stomach. "*You? You* want to stay single?" Her rapid, shallow breaths made her head spin. She was suddenly dining with a stranger. "I mean, what happened to our quest? And when did you discover you had the gift of permanent celibacy?"

Tom's brows drew together. "I wasn't exactly thinking in terms of celibacy, Jess."

A mild gasp escaped her lips.

"Whoa." Tom raised both his hands. "I mean, celibacy is part of not being married, of course. I know what the Word says. But staying single is not a fate worse than death either."

"Maybe not for you." An icy chill ran up her spine. "But I *want* a husband and children and—"

"A white-picket fence?" Tom grinned, and her heart sank like a rock. "Sorry. I'm not making fun of you, Jess. And I'm not trying to discourage you either. You'll meet the right guy." He loaded his fork with pasta—as if he hadn't just demolished her heart.

She couldn't drag her gaze from his face. She felt like screaming, "Look at me! What's wrong with me?" But she clamped her mouth shut. More than anything else, she had an urge to jump to her feet and run for the door. But what would Tom be left to conclude? "Well, if you don't want to be married, don't be."

Tom tapped his napkin to his chin and scrutinized her, his dark eyes narrowed. "I didn't say that either."

"Well, what exactly did you say?" She was trembling now. *Lord, help me!* She'd come so close to telling him in the truck she loved him. Too close. A chill raised the hairs on her arms. Her father's advice against women chasing men had been on the mark. She was thankful Tom had interrupted her little speech. He must've sensed what was coming, and this was his gentle way of letting her down easy.

"I'm saying what I'm saying." Tom shook his head. "I don't know what I'm saying anymore. What are you getting so uptight about?"

"I am *not* uptight!" Jess ground out the words between clenched teeth.

"Yeah, I can see that." Tom grunted and shook his head.

Jess blinked quickly to dry her eyes and looked across the room, her gaze settling on the gondola mural. They had never taken a sailing trip as Tom promised when he'd given her the porcelain boat. She loved that snowy Valentine's Day, sitting in the diner, sipping hot cocoa, and exchanging gifts. Theirs were never the typical, romantic gifts of lovers. They'd both known better than to cross that line. And she should've known better tonight.

Jess resumed eating. She'd not sulk like a child, laying bare to Tom more of her needy side.

Tom cleared his throat. "By the way, how did it go with Frank today?" The offhanded remark rolled off his tongue without effort. He was obviously being polite, making small talk. It wouldn't matter to him if she answered or totally changed the subject.

"Oh, we had lunch and talked. He's an interesting guy once you get to know him." Tom's smile slipped a bit, and she reveled in the small triumph. But who was she kidding? It was only his male ego rejecting the thought of Frank and her together. Just like Juan's ex—not wanting him and not wanting anybody else to have him. The disappointment she read on Tom's face had everything to do with Frank being his coworker and buddy. The two even made a game of comparing who had bigger muscles.

"Are you in the mood for Central Park tonight?" Tom inched his dish away. "You finished only half your dinner, but I could use the exercise."

Jess managed a smile. "Sure, why not?"

Yes, her father had been so right. But she'd make the most of this evening. End it on a high note. And if Tom had suspected she wanted more from him, she'd put his fears to rest.

fifteen

Tom rested his back against the park bench and stared up at the stars. No single male in his right mind would be this close to Jess and not kiss her. Except for a rare passerby and the sound of chattering crickets, they had this corner of the park to themselves. Jess looked more dazzling than he could remember. And as usual—he would do nothing about it.

"It's a beautiful night, isn't it?" Tom ran his gaze over her delicate profile and watched a slow smile curve her lips. Everything in him wanted to blurt out, "I love you." He clamped his jaw. Wouldn't that be appropriate? Say it, then fly off to California? To what end? At least if he left things as is, when he returned to New York on business, they'd slip back easily into their comfortable friendship.

"It's a gorgeous night. Perfect, really." Tipping her chin, Jess faced him fully. "How could you consider never getting married?" A worry line creased her brow. "Wouldn't tonight be even more perfect if you were with your one true love?"

Tom felt his heart drop. He clamped his hands behind his head and breathed in the scent of dewy grass. "You've always liked that expression."

"Which expression?" Jess slapped his knee playfully. "Are you making fun of me?"

"Uh-uh. But you're definitely partial to 'one true love.'"

"Oh, come on—call it what you like then." Jess fluffed her hair and tilted her chin.

Tom bit back a grin. Every time he thought he had her figured, Jess knocked him for a loop. He would've never guessed his simple statement over dinner could get her so riled. Why should she care whether or not he married? Unless she actually felt sorry for him? Shifting, Tom rested his elbows on his knees. "It's already a perfect night."

Jess inched closer to him and rested her hand on his forearm. His gut response was to pull away—move far and fast. His arm muscles tightened under her touch. "Wouldn't it be *more* perfect, I'm saying, if you were with your one true. All right—scratch that expression. Your significant other?" Jess laughed.

"It couldn't be more perfect than it is right now, Jess." Tom met her gaze. She was free to draw whatever conclusion she liked, but she didn't flinch.

Jess licked her sweet, upturned lips and sighed. "Well, I don't get it. You haven't answered my question." She drew back her hand, crossed her arms over her midsection, and looked off into the distance.

He gripped the edge of the wooden bench and shook his head. Of course she didn't get it. And she never would. Wasn't that why she started searching for Mr. Right on the Internet in the first place? "Listen, Jess—I meant to tell you. I'm probably—not probably—I've been offered a transfer at work, and I'm going to take it."

Jess stared, lips parted, face flushed. "You're moving?"

"Right. It'll be good for my—"

"Career?" Her voice was flat. Fiddling with the chain on her purse, her gaze lowered, her dark lashes hid her eyes from him. "How long have you known?"

Tom raked his fingers through his hair and shrugged. "I got the memo a couple of weeks back."

"And did you have to take it?" Her gaze snapped to his. A glint of anger seemed to flash in her eyes. "Didn't they give you a choice?"

"I had the option of staying here." *But this is killing me.* "I thought of all the reasons not to go, like—"

"Like inheriting your parents' rent-controlled apartment? Now there's a rare commodity in Manhattan."

Tom nodded. "That was one incentive." He drew another long breath. "But *you* were my biggest incentive to stay." *And to go.*

"Me?" Jess pointed to herself, eyes wide with mock surprise. "Your mathematical mind really factored me in?"

"Is that sarcasm?" Tom snorted a mild laugh. "For your information, our sixteen-year friendship did weigh heavily on my mind." *If only she knew how heavily.*

"And you concluded you can actually live without me?" Jess straightened her shoulders and batted her lashes, feigning indignation. "Where are you going?"

Tom brushed back a windblown strand of hair from her cheek. At least he'd leave guilt-free. Her reaction, though shocking, told him he was a lot more dispensable to her than he cared to admit. "San Diego."

"That far?" Jess nodded slowly. "Well, now you can finally go sailing. Remember the—"

"Boat I gave you? Yeah, I remember." Tom stood and extended his hand to her. Jess reached out, lacing her fingers with his, and got to her feet. He cleared his throat. "I'll be here for a couple more weeks. We'll plan a trip to Atlantic Beach maybe. What do you say?"

"Sure, that would be great." With her face raised to his, her sweet breath feathered his mouth. He stifled his impulse to plant one long, lingering kiss on her lips and cupped his hands loosely around her wrists.

Jess gave a shaky smile, which disappeared quickly. "I have to tell you something." Not a hint of playfulness remained in her voice. "But I don't know if this is bad timing—or what."

With his gaze still fastened on hers, Tom squared his shoulders. "Do you want to pray on it first?" Struck again by the same feeling that had hit him in the truck, his heart slammed against his ribs. He tightened his hands around her wrists, shoving away hope, yet still hoping. He had stood in this place too many times—waiting for a cue from Jess—a phrase, a look, a smile, anything to hang his heart onto.

"I–I don't think I need to pray on this."

Slipping his hands up her arms, he drew her closer. "Then tell me, Jess." He gave her a mild shake. "I thought we could tell each other anything."

A pang of guilt hit. Anything—except what he'd been carrying around in his heart all these years.

sixteen

Tom's steady gaze burned a wildfire through her. She had to tell him *now*. The thickness in her throat threatened to cut off her air. What would he think? After all these years as friends, Tom says he's moving and suddenly she says, "I love you"? He might see it as her last-ditch effort to hang onto him.

A tremor started in the pit of her stomach, rattling every nerve ending in her body. "Tom—" Jess closed her eyes, opened them. "It's what I—I was going to tell you in the truck."

Tom put more pressure on her arms, sending heat through her skin. "I'm listening, Jess."

"But you have to promise"—reaching up, she rested both her hands atop his solid shoulders—"you won't laugh."

A strand of brown hair fell forward on his forehead. His brows pulled together, emphasizing his dark eyes. The words stuck at the back of her throat. "I'm not laughing, Jess."

"I know. I know you're not." She drew a shaky breath. "Tom. . .what if I've. . .well, what if I've fallen in love. . . with you?"

Tom's gaze flashed from her eyes to her lips, making her heart drum harder. Jess lowered her lids, her eyes burning as she fought a tide of emotions, waiting for his response. Waiting. . .

She felt the pressure of Tom's fingers under her chin as he raised her face to his. "This isn't one of our guessing games? Is it, Jess?" Tom's brown-sugar gaze moved over her face slowly, melting her heart.

Her pulse sped up so quickly that she thought she might faint—or die—but she froze. "Do you want it to be? A guessing game?"

A solemn shadow passed over his eyes.

Jess felt herself trembling. "No—no, it's not a guessing game."

A hint of a smile crinkled the corners of his eyes. "Are you saying you're in love with me, Jess?"

Heat crawled up her neck, shooting into her cheeks, setting her aflame with embarrassment. But it was now or never. Tom was leaving. "Yes, that's what I'm—"

Her last word was swallowed in his kiss. Drinking in the warmth of his long-awaited kiss, Jess sank into his embrace, clutching his jacket. She'd always belonged in his arms.

"I'll stay, Jess." Tom's soft lips brushed against hers as he spoke. Raising his mouth from hers, he gazed into her eyes. "I only wanted to go to California to get—"

"Wait!" A dizzying current ran through her. Jess stiffened; her breaths came faster. She pressed her palms flat against his solid chest, putting distance between them. Oh, but it couldn't be true. Surely she was mistaken. Tom would never deceive her. Words tumbled through her head— *California. . .TC. . .West Coast. . . .* The horrid flashes of memory sucked the strength from her legs. "Tom, am I paranoid, or—" *Please, Lord, let me be mistaken. He'd never trick me, never make a fool of me.*

"What?" Frowning, Tom shook his head. "What is—"

"You don't, by any chance, use the handle TCTwo on—"

"Oh, I, um. . ." Tom nodded.

Jess gasped and broke free of his embrace. Her spine snapped straight.

"Jess." Tom raised his hands in a gesture of surrender. "Please don't get upset. I can explain—"

"Oh, no—no." She felt the color siphon from her face. "You wouldn't. You didn't." She spun, half walking, half running to the park's exit, leaving her dignity behind.

Jess heard his footsteps behind her. Tom closed the gap

between them quickly and grasped her arm. "Jess, it was a mistake. I wrote—"

Wresting her arm free from his grip, she twisted and glared at him. "Are you going to lie to me again? I told you my handle was Loves God." Licking her lips, she still tasted his kiss. The lingering warmth sent an ache to her heart. "You manipulated me, pretending to be my friend." She pushed her wayward hair from her face, turned, and scanned the avenue for a taxi. "You pretended to be my friend in E-mail and"—she waved her hands, hailing the cab—"and in person."

Tom slipped in front of her and took hold of her wrist. "Will you give me a chance to explain? Please, Jess, I—"

She drew back her hand, panting now. "Don't say another word. Don't!" Her lip trembled. What had she written in those E-mails? Forcing the memory made her stomach churn. How could he? The one man she'd trusted other than her father.

Jess opened the car door, dove into the waiting cab, and slammed it shut. She looked straight ahead, ignoring Tom standing at the curb, and sputtered her address to the cab driver.

Jess gritted her teeth as the car sped off. The day Tom left New York wouldn't come soon enough.

❧

Tom scanned the financials Frank dropped in front of him. His eyes read figures, but his mind registered nothing. "I'll have to look these over later." He snapped the folder shut and tossed it on the desk.

"Come on—let's have it." Frank dropped into the chair in front of his desk.

Tom lifted his gaze to him, studying his relaxed pose, as his blood pumped hot lava through his veins. Frank couldn't possibly possess the unmitigated gall to expect a tell-all. "How'd your week's vacation go?"

Frank studied his fingernails for a second, looked up, and smiled. "Great. Fantastic." Leaning back in his chair, he ran his hand down his tie. "I saw Jess a couple of times." A smug grin curled his lips. "I'm telling you—I feel so much better since she and I had a heart-to-heart."

Tom stood and scrubbed his hand across his jaw. "Is that right?" Gritting his teeth, he shoved his hands into his pockets.

"Definitely." Smiling, Frank nodded slowly.

Hardly breathing, his gaze met the bold challenge in Frank's eyes. The guy was pushing for a conversation about Jess. But he wouldn't give him one—give him the opportunity to gloat.

"I'm transferring to California." Tom scanned the office he'd worn like a home away from home for the past eight years. He'd miss it, but—

"Whoa." Frank raised his hands in a familiar gesture that usually made him laugh. But since last week, nothing brought a smile to his face. A solid week and a day, and his phone messages to Jess had gone unanswered. He wasn't about to walk into Flavors and risk a scene at her place of work. "Anyway, I recommended you to Elliot for the promotion. Not that you're qualified, but you always liked the view in here."

Frank gave him a half-smile. "You know you're running, right?"

Tom snorted a laugh. "Nah, there's nothing to run from anymore." He shrugged, sat down, and opened the folder. "I'd better get started on these before I have no job."

"Which office are you transferring to?"

"Didn't Jess tell you?" Tom cleared his throat. Of course, *he* wouldn't be the topic of discussion at their little powwows. He had lived a whole minute believing Jess was in love with him. But she had easily fallen out of love with him. *Not real love, Jess.* "San Diego."

"Man." Looking down, he wagged his head. And for a second he thought he read disappointment in Frank's demeanor. But his discernment left quite a bit to be desired.

"How long before you leave?"

Tom rocked back in his chair. "A couple of weeks. Mid-June maybe."

"Much as I love the view in this office," Frank stood abruptly and puffed out a breath, "and I thank you for your recommendation, by the way, I don't want to see you go, Buddy."

Tom tapped his fingers on the desktop. "Do me a favor. If you—when you see, Jess—" He pulled in a breath. Just the right man to deliver the message. "Never mind. I've got to look at these now." He flipped open the folder, dismissing Frank with the motion. Mercifully, his coworker took the cue and strode across the room.

He waited until he heard the snap of the door behind Frank, then grabbed the phone. He had two things to accomplish—a request that Elliot get him out of New York as soon as possible—and an apology to Jess.

Tom punched his boss's extension. There was enough in Jess's background to give her reason to distrust, but he'd not be another cog in the wheel of suspicion, pushing her to be even more wary.

If Jess continued to ignore his calls, there was always E-mail or a letter. But in either case she could delete it or tear it to shreds.

One way or another, he had to speak to her once more, face-to-face. And then he would go.

❧

Jess looked down at her battle-scarred hands. Three cuts and two burns in ten days. That had to be a record. She slanted a glance at Juan, who was dusting flour off his hands. "You've been such a big help this week."

"Nah, nothing. What about the bad weeks I had—when Maria left? You did triple duty to cover for me." He winked. "Juan doesn't forget."

Jess managed a smile. "I'm not judging, Juan, but how could Maria have left you?" She hung the last pan on the hook above the stove and untied her apron.

"It's not her fault. I took Maria for granted." Juan swiped his heavy key chain off the counter and shook his head. "Some of us don't know what we have till we lose it."

A pang of sadness jabbed her heart. "Well, I'm just sorry you two lost each other." Jess shrugged. There were no answers. Only questions. "You two seemed perfect for one another."

"Aha, like you and Tom," Juan said before exiting the kitchen.

Jess snapped off the lights and followed him into the dining room. Juan didn't understand all she'd been through. She had risked saying "I love you" to the one man on earth she trusted with her heart. "We're not friends anymore, Juan."

Jess stepped outside behind him, inhaling the rain-scented air, and closed and locked the door to Flavors.

"You were friends?" Juan's tanned face broke into a smile. "You were never friends." He took a few steps backward, saluted, and said, "Adios."

Jess stared after him. She opened her mouth to call his name. Of course Tom *had* been her friend. Just because she'd caught Tom in a lie—an awful lie—it didn't negate what they had before. Or did it? Perhaps this wasn't the first time Tom had seen fit to pretend he was somebody he was not.

Jess walked slowly past the darkened storefronts. What was Juan insinuating with that comment? Had he seen or heard something more about Tom that she was unaware of?

Not that it mattered. One lie was one too many.

Turning the corner, Jess shuddered in midstep as she nearly crashed into Frank.

seventeen

Tom zipped his suitcase, hefted it off the bed, and carried it into the living room. He dropped the bag on the floor beside the packed cartons of his other worldly possessions and groaned.

Too bad Elliot hadn't agreed to let him leave for the West Coast earlier. It would've given him a valid excuse not to attend Corinne's wedding. Much as he was happy for Rick and Corinne, he'd be forced to see Jess tomorrow, something he'd realized wasn't best.

Cupping his hand to the back of his aching neck, he shook his head. Jess would avoid him like the plague at the reception. But by now Corinne might know the score and see the wisdom of not seating them together—he hoped.

Tom strode into the kitchen, grabbed a can of iced tea from the refrigerator and sat at the table for a much-needed break. He gazed out the window, looking out onto the maze of steel skyscrapers that was Manhattan. He shouldn't miss the mayhem of the concrete jungle—but he would. And he'd miss Jess. But his heart had hit rock bottom. He could only go up from there.

Days ago he'd decided to stop phoning Jess, stop leaving messages of apology. It was hopeless, he knew. She wouldn't forgive him. Not because he'd committed the unforgivable sin, but because she'd allowed herself to cross a dangerous commitment line, and she needed to step back, run away. He could do nothing more. Only the Lord could change her heart.

And yet Jess trusted Frank enough to continue seeing him.

147

Tom drummed his fingers on the tabletop. His colleague enjoyed rubbing that fact in his face. According to Jess's E-mail, she feared he wanted to deck Frank when he'd seen them together in Flavors. She should've seen him yesterday, his fists clenched and his desire full-blown.

Tom sighed. Since when did the wrath of man produce the righteousness of God? Would decking Frank bring Jess to her senses? No, his relationship with the Lord was far more important than satisfying his fleshly desires.

He shook his head, switched his gaze to the laptop, and hit the key to close the financial document he'd been working on this morning. Maybe he'd write one last E-mail to Jess. If he changed his mind about sending it, there was always the DELETE button.

Tom typed in his password. This time he would use his real identity, though the chances of Jess actually opening and reading his message were minuscule. "Give me the words, Lord."

Dear Jess,

I'm writing this even knowing you'll probably never read it. I'm sorry you've chosen to ignore my phone messages and sorrier that you've chosen not to forgive me.

I realize you had it tough growing up without a mom and that you struggle with trust issues. Again, I'm without excuse for having deceived you in E-mail. (I did, however, use my real initials. My middle name is Christopher, same as my dad's, though you wouldn't know that since I'd never before used it.) But, Jess, please know my motives were pure. I don't want to go off to California feeling I've added to your burden in any way.

The first time I e-mailed Loves God, I had no idea it was you. Do you remember, Jess? You gave me your handle after the fact. I realize that doesn't absolve me from what took place once you told me you were Loves God, but at least try to understand my motive. You sounded down, and I only wanted to help.

There is one thing I've kept hidden from you for the past sixteen years. You accused me of lying with regard to the "TC" situation, and if the omission of truth constitutes a lie, I'm afraid I stand accused. And here it is, Jess.

I've loved you from the moment I saw you. Something happened to my heart that first day of class in junior year. (If this sounds pathetic to you, imagine me, carrying this around for so long, trying to deny it.) I knew right then and there you were the only one for me. But I've finally tossed all my defense mechanisms into the trash. And that's what makes it okay for me to stay single. The Lord knows it, I know it, and if you bother to read this, you'll know it too.

That's all the truth I have to tell. Except when you said in the park, "What if I've fallen in love with you?" I was about to ask you to marry me. I love you. I doubt there'll come a day when I stop loving you. Even Linda saw it that day in Flavors when you were with Jim. I guess Linda read it on my face, like so many others have—yet you've been blind to it all these years. In retrospect, I realize I needed to hide behind TC to find the courage to tell you.

I know what you think of me, Jess, but please don't allow my behavior to color your future. You have a great future. God's plans for you are good. You'll have a husband, and children, and even a white-picket fence, because you deserve those things. I guess you were right about me. I had it easy growing up. My parents thought I was God's gift to humankind, and my sisters—need I say more? So I don't know what it's like to have been abandoned by a parent, but losing you has taught me a lot. I'll never again waste time worrying about my ego—too afraid to say what's on my heart for fear of the other person's response.

There is one more thing, and I can only hope you won't perceive this as jealousy. But Frank is aware of my feelings for you and has been for a long time. So I find his sudden interest in you suspect. His motives may be pure, of course, and I don't want to believe he's using you to compete with me. Just keep praying, and I know the Lord will be faithful to reveal all truth.

I'm sure I'll see you tomorrow (Sunday) at Corinne's wedding, but I doubt you'll be in any mood to speak with me; hence, the purpose of this E-mail. But don't worry about having to see me again. I'll be off on a flight to San Diego the following day.

Take care, Jess. I'll be praying for you.

All my love,
Tom

Jess picked shredded tissues from the desk and carpet and tossed them into the wastebasket. She had cried alone on the anniversary of her father's death. Those tears were valid. But except for cuts and burns, she'd held it together in Flavors for two straight weeks. The Lord had been her strength. He'd gotten her through. She had survived.

If only she hadn't succumb to the temptation to open Tom's E-mail.

Jess strode to her room, flicked on the light, and dropped to the edge of her bed. She fell back against the pillows and stared at the ceiling. She didn't need a glimpse in the mirror to know her face was a swollen mess. But she had to find a way to look presentable for Corinne's wedding tomorrow.

Turning onto her side, Jess drew her knees to her chest, grabbed her pillow, and stifled another sob. All these years. . .

Why hadn't she recognized Tom was in love with her? How could she face Tom tomorrow? But as a bridesmaid, there was no getting out of the wedding now.

Jess rolled onto her other side and looked at her gown, hanging outside her closet door. *Silver.* She couldn't help but choke back a laugh. Corinne had a flare for glitzy. And the slit up the side ended just above her knee. What would Tom think? Oh, what did it matter?

He had loved her from the start, he wrote. And puppy love was sweet. But Tom had never told her as much until she'd said it first. In fact he'd made plans to leave New York, leave her. What kind of love was that? So much love that Tom was going off to the West Coast all the same. And his warning about Frank. . .

Tom need not worry. Being virtually alone for the past two weeks had taught her a spiritual lesson she'd never forget. The Lord had been her comforter and her strength. And finally she'd arrived where her father wanted her to be. She no longer needed to be married, though she still wanted to be. A big difference.

Jess sat up slowly and scrubbed her hands over her face. The question she'd come to despise and fear loomed large in her thoughts again. Was she just like her mom—the woman she never knew, but whose genes and DNA she carried with her wherever she went?

Whenever she'd broached the subject with her father, he was vague, until his sad countenance at the mention of her mother's name made her stop asking altogether. "Mom had her share of problems, Jess," he'd say. "But don't we all?"

"Yes, Daddy, don't we all?" Even if she married Tom, she'd never know if she'd walk out the door one fine day. Act as crazy as her mother had. The thought made her too afraid to unlock the wooden box her father had kept in his room. He said there were some papers in it and, if anything should happen to him, to open it when she was ready. Ready?

Jess's gaze shot to her closet. No matter how far back on the shelf she stuffed the box, it was never far enough away from her thoughts. But if she opened it, she might see herself.

She rose from the bed slowly and walked across the floor as if on eggs. She slid open the closet door, ran her gaze up over her wardrobe, and scanned the shelf. Perhaps she wouldn't find it among the haphazard remnants of her life.

Jess moved aside two shoe boxes full of old cards and letters. And there it stood, almost beckoning her. She swallowed hard, reached high, and grasped it with her fingertips.

Sitting in the armchair, she ran her hand over the dusty wood. "Lord, if I shouldn't unlock this, give me a sign. If it's more than I can handle—"

Jess turned and pulled open the nightstand drawer. That's how she'd know. If she couldn't find the key, she couldn't open it tonight. She swished aside a bottle of perfume and some soaps, and her heart did a somersault. "Oh, no, it's here."

Her hands shook as she inserted the small key into the lock. What if there were medical papers, stating that her mother had a breakdown? Jess lifted the lid slowly.

She bit her lip as hot tears slipped down her cheeks. She picked up the photo of her smiling mother. It wasn't the first picture she'd ever seen of her, but certainly the clearest. They looked so much alike.

Jess placed it on the desk. For a box no larger than ten inches across, her father had managed to store quite a bit neatly. She carefully unfolded a yellowed document—her parents' marriage certificate. Putting that atop her mother's photo, her breath caught when she saw her name scrawled on an envelope in her father's handwriting.

Forgetting her fears, she tore open the side, slipped out the lined paper, and heard a *clink* on the floor. Bending, she picked up the antique-looking gold and diamond ring, slipped it on her finger, and began to read.

My dearest daughter, Jessica,

If you're reading this, I'm already with the Lord in glory. No need to stain your beautiful face with tears. Although as strong as you tried to be for both of us, you've always been sensitive. So go ahead and cry if need be. I'm not around to tell you to quit the girly-girl tears. I was only trying to protect you when I said that. But I also know I made a lot of mistakes raising you.

You probably found the ring I enclosed with this letter. It belonged to my mother, your grandma Stewart. You were so young when she passed away, but I wish you would have gotten to know her. You're so much like her, and you can be proud of that. She was a loving, sensitive woman, although she had a temper at times. Ha. And when she wanted something, there was no stopping her. But besides all that, I'm giving you the ring in hopes that you'll wear it when you marry Tom.

Jess clutched her blouse, struggling for air.

I can just imagine the shocked look in your beautiful blue eyes. I know I hounded you about a career and being independent. But you accomplished all those things long ago. And if you're reading this letter for the first time, I know you're not yet married to Tom. The reason? The same courage it took to open this box, to read this letter, is what you need to say yes to Tom. Has that big lug asked yet? Ha. If not, he will. I saw it in his eyes the minute he walked in the door, baseball mitt tucked under his arm. I couldn't hope for a better husband for my precious little girl. That man is head over heels in love with you, Jess. No doubt about it.

"Oh, Daddy, you don't understand." Jess's shoulders shook with a sob.

And now I come to the subject of your mother. I never did want to go over the details with you, Sweetie. I couldn't stand it. I couldn't stand myself for losing her. But it was all my fault. We were married two years before Angela got pregnant with you. During those years I put your mother through hell on earth. I wasn't the man you know as "Daddy." I was out carousing till all hours and doing all sorts of wrong things. Angela put up with me until you were born. And then she couldn't seem to take anymore. She tried, Jess. She really did. But one Tuesday morning in March, when you were about two months old, she told me she was leaving. I guess I was hung over, because her words didn't sink in until days then weeks passed.

My mother, bless her soul, came to help. And that's when I straightened out my act right quick. But it was too late by then. Angela was gone, and till this Christmas Day 2001 I still don't know where she is or whether she's dead or alive.

I hope you don't hate me, darling Jess. You were the light of my life. You're the reason I started going to church and working two jobs. I knew I had to get it right. That you lost your mother because of me and the things I'd done to push her away. But none of those things will happen with you and Tom! Don't think I didn't know what you were really asking when you talked about your mom. But please don't be afraid. Tom will never give you reason to run. He loves God, and he loves you. And who can blame him? You're the best and brightest, and you always will be.

Daddy loves you, Jess. Tom loves you too. And most of all God loves you! And you can tell Tom he'd better name your firstborn son after me. I deserve as much for giving him my blessing to marry you.

I'd better end here. I've been hiding in my bedroom from

you and Tom, but now it's time to enjoy Christmas.

Love you forever,

Daddy

Holding her father's letter to her chest, Jess lay on her bed and cried until she fell asleep.

eighteen

Gazing at the lovely bride sitting across from her in the limo, Jess smiled. "I'm so happy for you, Corinne." Oh, to say those words and mean them from the bottom of her heart. Finally to be content as the bridesmaid, knowing God was in charge and all was well with her soul.

"Thanks, Jess. But I should've thought twice before choosing that gown for you." Corinne tilted her chin. "You're going to steal the show."

Jess shook her head. "Not at all." She tugged at the shimmering silver material, which fit too snug to her skin for comfort. Somehow she'd actually gained the few pounds she needed to fill out the dress. Tiramisu to the rescue.

"Stop fussing, Jess." Corinne pushed at her veil as if it were her wild red hair. "I know you're used to conservative, but you look like a movie star in that thing, and it's really not revealing."

"She does look like a movie star." Brenda, the matron-of-honor, wore something no less sparkling, but it was gold.

Jess laughed. "Oh, stop it, you two. You're marrying a great guy today, Corinne." She turned her head. "And you. You don't need any more attention than what you already get from Mike."

Brenda's ivory-skinned face lit with a shy smile. "Now it's your turn, Jess. You're the last hold-out."

"Yes." Jess switched her gaze to the side window. "It's my turn." But being ready to become Tom's wife—being so in love with Tom her heart hurt—didn't change what he'd written in his E-mail. He was leaving, despite his claim that he loved her.

"I hear Marilyn's pregnant again." Corinne fluffed the lacy material of her gown. "That's one busy lady."

"Yep." Jess rubbed her arms. "I'm freezing in this car."

"Too much A/C. It's a beautiful day." Corinne hit the button on the console, and the electric window slid down. "I want to show off a bit anyway. Nobody can see me through this tinted glass."

Jess smiled and lifted her face to the sunshine streaming into the car. "Oh, that feels good."

"Excuse me." Brenda grabbed her left hand. "Where'd you get this ring?"

Corinne jolted forward in her seat. "Let me see that." Her green eyes narrowed. "Have you been holding out on us?"

"No, no. It was my grandmother's." Jess looked from one face to the other. "I promise."

"Wow! It's gorgeous." Brenda twisted the ring this way and that. The sun reflected into the diamond, sending multi-colored hues shooting around the car.

Corinne coughed. "But you'd better get it off *that* finger. All the guys are going to think you're engaged. Especially one guy."

The words jabbed her heart and sent flutters to her stomach. "Yes, well, that *one guy* is leaving for San Diego tomorrow. Moving away. As Juan would say, 'Adios.'"

Corinne gasped. Brenda stared, mute.

Jess pushed a smile to her face. "Well, you didn't expect Tom to wait around for me forever, did you?" What she intended as humor hung in the car, wreaking of sarcasm. Both her friends exchanged glances.

"Hey, just tell him not to go." A tendril of Corinne's red hair popped out from under her veil. She closed the window.

"Yes, Corinne's right. You have to tell him," Brenda chimed in with conviction.

Jess shook her head. "I haven't a tenth of the courage of either of you. That's why—"

"You're not married to Tom yet." Corinne flashed an apologetic smile. "Sorry. But in a way I'm not sorry. In fact, I think I'll dedicate a song to the two of you at the reception."

Jess's spine snapped straight. "Don't you dare, Corinne. I'll never forgive you." She gave Brenda a sidelong glance. "And stop smirking, you."

The sly look on Corinne's face made her pulse trip. Like a loose cannon, the bride had always been the type to do or say as she pleased. Corinne tilted her head. "Maybe I'll have them play "Endless Love." Anyone looking at you two together can see it."

Jess felt her nails digging harder into her palms. "Honestly. Promise you won't do that."

Corinne frowned. "Sorry, Jess—I was only kidding. Really." She reached across the seat and patted her hand. "I'm not a very good matchmaker at that. I tripped over Rick for five years before it dawned on me that I was in love with him. I'm thankful to the Lord that the feeling was mutual."

Brenda laughed. "Yeah, Jess, we were kidding." She cleared her throat. "Still, if you asked Tom not to leave, I'm positively sure he wouldn't."

"Well, I'd never ask him any such thing." Jess settled back against the soft leather seat. Her father's letter didn't change what he'd said to her face—she shouldn't have to chase any man, not even Tom. She'd had to overcome her own demons—fear being the worst of them. But Tom had a few of his own.

The Lord had revealed more truth to her in the past two months than in all her years combined.

Tom would have to make the move this time—and not the move to California.

❧

The bridal march commenced. Tom turned toward the back of the church in unison with the other attendees. His gaze froze on Jess. He swallowed hard as he watched her move smoothly up the aisle, Rick's brother at her side. With each step, her gown shone against her skin, lighting her gorgeous eyes.

Tom squared his shoulders. He shouldn't have come here today. A heaviness in the center of his chest made looking at Jess unbearable.

As she passed, she raised her gaze, and her cool blue eyes met with his for a split second. He ran his hand down his tie and looked toward the back of the church. He might actually suffocate before he got through this ordeal.

After watching Brenda's solemn walk up the aisle, he smiled when Corinne practically skipped toward her groom. The enthusiastic bride wasn't afraid to show the world how much she loved Rick.

The more he'd thought about it—and he'd had plenty of time to think these past weeks—the more sense it made that Jess's profession of love in Central Park had been spoken on a whim. He could forgive that. He'd told her he was going away, and panic would be her first response to being left alone.

The minister's words penetrated his thoughts. Tom shifted in his seat.

"Love is patient and kind. Love is not jealous or boastful or proud or rude. Love does not demand its own way. Love is not irritable, and it keeps no record of when it has been wronged."

His gaze strayed, resting on Jess again. *Get me through this, Lord.* He could congratulate Corinne and Rick at the church doors, give them the envelope, and apologize for being unable to attend the reception. The plan taking shape in his mind brought him a measure of comfort. They'd never miss him at a hundred-and-fifty-person reception.

At the feel of a nudge at his back, Tom turned his head. He saw Frank sitting behind him, smiling.

Tom's muscles tensed. He hated the feeling of not trusting.

He nodded a greeting, turned, and faced the front. He should've counted on Frank's being here today. The last straw, the final blow, would be if Frank was here as Jess's date.

"Love never gives up, never loses faith," the preacher said. "Love is always hopeful and endures through every circumstance."

Never gives up. Tom clenched his jaw. He wouldn't beg off from the reception. He'd stand and take the brunt of it, come what may.

The bride and groom looked into each other's eyes, repeated their vows, and exchanged rings. The weight in Tom's chest grew heavier. At every wedding, he and Jess were standing at the altar. And finally he was kissing his beautiful bride, the woman he'd never stop loving.

But unless something miraculous happened today, his dreams would be just that—hopes unrealized.

❧

"Hello, Jess."

Jess's pulse zoomed before she looked up. "Hi, there."

Tom glanced at the white card in his hand, which listed seating arrangements. "Looks like this is my table."

A smile tugged at her lips, despite the resignation she detected in his voice. "Well, have a seat." Jess indicated the chair beside hers at the table for twelve and shot a glance at the couple seated at the far end. She was glad they were too busy chatting to care about an introduction.

This might be their last time together or the beginning of their future.

Tom hesitated a moment. Jess held her breath, waiting, hoping, and considering the hard feelings between them.

After a quick glance around the dining room and a brief smile, Tom sat and unbuttoned his suit jacket.

Jess released a long breath, her senses awakening to Tom's clean lime scent. She'd been foolish for making a big deal of the TC incident. Her father's letter was all that mattered now. Tom loved her. He had always loved her. She scanned his serious profile, not wholly convinced of the fact. "By the way, I read your E-mail."

Turning, his face reflected mild surprise. Her last-ditch attempt seemed to make no impact on him. "Really? I didn't think you would." His voice was flat. Her jittery stomach told her the evening couldn't end soon enough for him.

Jess sat up straighter, determined to get it right this time. "I'm sorry I didn't return your phone calls. I needed time to think."

Tom shrugged. "Understandable, Jess. No big deal."

Yes, it's a very big deal. She wanted to punch the walls. They needn't be formal with one another. But here they were, acting like strangers. "I overreacted to the Love Online incident. I'm sorry."

"I'm sorry, too." Tom ran his gaze over her quickly. "Let's forget it."

He was leaving. Jess squeezed her hands together on the tabletop. The solid walls around him blocked her from asking him to stay. Corinne and Brenda and all her friends were wrong. Yes, even her father.

"You look beautiful, Jess."

A spark of hope sent warmth through her. "Thanks. You're looking quite good yourself." From the corner of her eye, she caught sight of Frank heading toward their table. Jess sighed. *Oh, please, not now.*

"Hey, hey, I finally made it." Frank's voice immediately severed the delicate threads holding whatever remained of them together.

Tom's smile vanished. He flicked a glance at Frank, then back at her.

Jess shook her head, trying to answer the questions and erase the hurt she read in Tom's eyes. She shot Frank a look.

"So where are you sitting?"

Frank jerked his thumb in the direction behind them. "I *was* sitting over there. Made a deal with a lady who was supposed to be sitting here, and"—Frank dropped into the vacant seat beside hers—"we switched." He laughed.

Tom shook his head.

Caught in the thick maze of tension between the two, Jess prayed the floor would open up and swallow her whole. She turned her head, focusing on Tom. "Are you leaving tomorrow?"

"Hey, Buddy." Frank leaned past her. "Tomorrow? I didn't know that."

Tom's mouth lifted in a cynical grin.

Holding the back of Tom's chair with her right hand, she pressed her fingers into the wood. *I love you, Tom. This is a misunderstanding.*

"Yeah, I'll be out of here before you know it," Tom said, staring down at the table.

"Too bad." Frank rested his hand on her wrist. Jess hesitated to pull away for fear of rousing Tom's attention.

Tom turned his head, dropped his gaze to the table, and nodded slowly. *Too late.*

He lifted his gaze to Frank. "Why do you ask? Are you going to miss me or something?" The bridled anger in his tone made her pulse kick up.

Jess dragged her foot under the table, searching for Frank's leg to give him a swift kick. Frank had to be daft not to sense the boiling undercurrent. Jess forced a laugh. "Didn't the bride look gorgeous?"

Neither of the men budged. Frank smiled. "Well, what do you think?"

In one quick motion, Jess slipped her hand out from under Frank's. "This place is lovely. I hear the food—"

"What do I think? I think you should be happy." Tom

leaned past her, closer to Frank, as if her chair were vacant. "You'll get my office, and you'll get—"

"Oh, come on, you guys." Jess swallowed past the rising panic in her throat. "You know you'll both miss each other."

"Excuse me." Tom pushed back from the table and stood. "I'd better get some air."

Jess watched him stride away, her heart sinking with his every step. She spun in her chair toward Frank, her jaw clenched. She took deep breaths until she thought she could speak without later regretting what she said. "You know, it's not right—you—practically coming onto me when Tom's here."

Frank rested his cheek against his fist. "I'm sorry, Jess, but I have only the most honorable intentions."

"Is that right? You may not know it, but I'm sure Tom interprets your *honorable intentions* as outright flirting."

Frank leaned back in his chair, shaking his head. "Tom's never said as much to me."

Jess felt her spine stiffen. "Maybe Tom's too much of a gentleman to say anything." She stopped for another breath, which did nothing to calm her. "But I know Tom. I know that even if Tom's hurting, he's too deep to push himself on others or try to control them."

"Yeah, that's what I think too." Frank grinned.

Jess glared at him. "Y–you don't act like it. It appears as if you're intentionally trying to hurt him." She dropped her gaze to the table, her throat and eyes burning. "I'm not suggesting you like me as anything more than a friend, Frank, but honestly—"

"Oh, but I do. I love you, and I love Tom, like a sister and brother."

Jess's gaze snapped to his. Why blame Frank? It was all her fault—playing hide-and-seek with her emotions when Tom asked her forgiveness. Ignoring him when she should've forgiven him on the spot, wrapped in his strong arms. "Then you'll have to forgive my outburst. I think I—"

"Should go after Tom." Frank jutted his chin. "He's on the terrace, you know."

Jess frowned, pushed back from the table, and stood. "I don't know what makes you tick, Frank, but I—"

"Oh, Jess, I was only trying to light a fire under Tom." Frank groaned. "If I went about it the wrong way, please forgive me. But I know how much Tom loves you." He smiled. "And I know how much you love him."

Her jaw hung ajar for a moment. "I think I have to go to Tom." Jess pivoted and headed for the double doors, her heart drumming in her ears.

nineteen

Jess twisted the shiny brass knob on the glass-paned door. She stepped outside onto the wooden planks and closed the door behind her gently. Clamping her hands behind her back, she observed Tom from a distance.

He stood facing the ocean, arms resting on the terrace guardrail. His profile, dark against the moonlight, made her senses tingle with excitement. A light breeze combed his thick brown hair. She was not afraid to say, "I love you."

She neared him on tiptoes, though he probably couldn't hear her approaching over the sound of roaring waves crashing along the shoreline.

Jess stopped several feet behind him. Her lips curved in a smile. Had she loved him from the moment their eyes met—as Tom said he loved her? Now she couldn't recall a day she hadn't been in love with him. His powerful presence had always drawn her. She had always preferred him above all others.

Drawing a deep breath of the salty night air, she felt as fearless as Frank—who'd nearly laid down his life to see them together. If Tom still chose to leave, one truth would remain.

The Lord, knowing their hearts, had orchestrated each event until they'd both arrived at this moment in time. He held their future in His capable hands.

"Hi, Jess," Tom said, without turning to her.

"Did you hear me?" Jess moved to the railing and stood alongside him.

"No." Tom turned his head. His dark gaze, as gentle as a caress, captured hers. "But nobody smells as nice as you do."

Gazing into his eyes, the anger she saw at the table was gone. Her heart ached as she drank in the comfort of his nearness. Would he really go away tomorrow? "And nobody's ever given me better counsel than you." She smiled.

"Hmm. What does that mean?" Tom's brows pulled together. And she even loved his frown.

"Aha." Staring out at the Atlantic, reflecting the big silvery moon and pounding the jetties, she was hit again by the enormous power of God. The Lord could do anything—change hearts and minds in an instant. "You've forgotten our outburst in Bible class, haven't you?" Jess gave him a sidelong glance.

Tom ran his gaze over her face slowly. "It's possible. But I doubt I've forgotten much of anything we've done together."

His ready confession made her heart skip beats. Jess turned, facing him fully. "Proverbs 27:9—do you remember? Mr. Baylor's class?" She couldn't restrain a grin.

"Oh, yes, now it's all coming back." Tom clucked his tongue. "Didn't that verse cost me dearly?"

"I'll say." Jess laughed. Tom ran his fingers over her cheek, tucking a wayward strand of hair behind her ear. "Y–you paid by scrubbing the schoolhouse floors on a Saturday—when you needed to practice for a big game."

Jess watched a familiar smile curve his tempting mouth. Her heart overflowed with love for him. Tom *had* loved her from the day they'd met. He'd done so in his quiet way, never asking anything in return.

Yet he had only said "I love you" to her face as her friend. His E-mail counted for something. But now she longed for more.

Tom tipped his head. "I know that verse. 'Ointment and perfume rejoice the heart.' " He nodded slowly. "And you always made my heart rejoice, Jess."

"Did I?" She held her breath. Dare she let herself believe he'd utter them now? But he glanced out at the wild sea, his jaw set.

Jess straightened her shoulders. " 'So doth the sweetness of a man's friend by hearty counsel,' the proverb goes on to say." She reached out hesitantly and took hold of his strong hands. "You've been a sweet friend, Tom, and you've given me hearty counsel."

Tom raised her left hand to his lips and pressed a kiss to her palm. "Jess, I—" His chest rose and fell with a deep breath. He brushed his thumb over the ring on her finger. "It's beautiful."

"Thanks." She slipped her hands from his grasp and held fast to the railing. They both faced the ocean now, together, but alone. "Is that what you really wanted to say about the ring, Tom?"

"No." He cleared his throat. "I wanted to ask where you got it. Who gave it to you. And why that ex-friend of mine is slobbering all over you, when I'll be out of his way by tomorrow." There was a hard edge to his voice. "That's what I wanted to say."

Jess tilted her chin. "You wrote in your E-mail that you've changed, Tom. You said you'd speak your mind from now on, regardless of how you thought the other person would respond."

"I know what I wrote, Jess." His iron will came through in his voice and in the rigid set of his broad shoulders. "And you think I've failed?"

"Yes. Insofar as you didn't ask all the things you wanted to." Jess felt her arms stiffen at her sides. She clenched her shaky hands and stomped one high-heeled foot against the wooden planks. *Say it, Tom—say it!*

"Okay, let's start with the ring. Who gave it to you?"

Jess glanced at the precious heirloom on her finger. "It was my grandmother's. I—I just found it last night, though it was never lost." Her voice came out a hoarse whisper.

"Your grandmother's?"

"Yes. I discovered it, along with a letter from my father, in the wooden lockbox he used to keep in his room. He said after he was gone, I should open it when I was ready."

Tom reached out, and suddenly she was in his arms, her face pressed against his solid chest. "I'm sorry, Jess. I guess it was better if I hadn't asked at all. Because it doesn't matter—"

"What?" Jess broke free of the short-lived respite of his embrace. She tugged at the waistline of her gown, shuddering, suddenly feeling exposed. "It doesn't matter?"

"No. It doesn't." Tom took a step toward her.

Jess stepped back. "And—and Frank, *slobbering all over me.* . ."

Tom closed the small gap between them. "I guess I'll have a talk with Frank about that later."

"Oh, please, don't bother. Frank only did it to make you jealous." Seeing the amusement in Tom's eyes, Jess gritted her teeth.

"I always knew that guy was a nut case." Tom laughed.

Jess found herself with her back pressed against the cold railing and Tom gazing down into her face. He sobered, and his dark eyes held a secret expression. Over the pounding surf, music from the reception hall drifted to her ears like a taunt. "That Corinne is—is *ridiculous.*" She squeezed her eyes shut. His nearness was a much more dangerous taunt.

"Corinne? Why?"

"That *stupid* song." Jess shook her head. If things had turned out differently, the song would've sounded beautiful in her ears. "I—I made her promise not to play it."

"Hmm. There's a rumor going around like that." Tom frowned. "And I thought to myself, if Corinne was too intimidated to have the band play it, then I would."

"Who—what—?" Staring into his handsome face, she bit her lip to stifle a gasp.

❧

"On my way in." Tom wound his arms around her tiny

waist, locking his hands behind her back. Her moonlit eyes widened. She opened her mouth as if to speak. "I spoke with Nick."

"Nick?" Jess licked her lips. She didn't blink.

"Nick's the bandleader." Tom bit back a grin. "And I said, 'Nick, I'm so in love with that woman over there.' I pointed to you. 'You've got to play "Endless Love" for us, because there's no chance we'll get over each other this side of heaven.'" He felt Jess trembling, watched a shaky smile grace her gorgeous face.

"Tom. . ." Tears spilled down her cheeks.

Tom cleared his throat. "And Nick says—mind you—in the worst Brooklyn accent I've ever heard, 'Hey, why doncha ask her ta marry ya?'"

Jess's porcelain shoulders shook with quiet laughter. "And what did you say, Tom?"

"Well, you know me. Never have been a risk-taker."

Smiling, Jess ran her fingers through his hair. "That isn't true. You skated down that steep garage—"

"Ah, that was only to impress you."

Resting both her hands on his shoulders, her blue gaze captured his. "Are you going to impress me again, Tom?"

He shrugged. "Only if asking you to marry me will impress you. Otherwise I—"

"But you've changed. You can't care how I respond."

"Hmm. You have me there." Tom released his hold on her. He dropped down to one knee, looked up into her sparkling eyes, and pressed her delicate hands. "Jessica Stewart, I love you with all my heart. I always have, and I always will. I'm asking you to marry me. Please say yes, or you'll be solely responsible for my never taking another risk."

Tom stood and faced her, smiling.

Jess expelled a breath. "Oh, even if I weren't madly in love with you, I would've had to say yes. Daddy enclosed this ring in his letter, with strict instructions to marry you."

"What? And you made me get down on one knee?" Tom crushed her to himself and laughed. "Dean always could read me. Did he know I was in love with you?"

"Yes—madly." Jess giggled.

Tom shook his head. "And since when was Dean ever wrong?"

"Never." Jess tilted her chin.

Tom's lips came down to meet hers. He kissed her with a passion borne of years of waiting. He pushed out of his mind the noises coming from behind them, until he could no longer ignore the fracas. Drawing back reluctantly, he looked into Jess's face, watching her eyes widen.

Tom turned.

Frank, Corinne, Rick, Marilyn, and Keith stood side-by-side grinning and applauding.

Corinne planted a hand on her hip. "I knew you'd get all the attention on my day, Missy."

"Does this mean I don't get your office?" Frank scowled.

Tom turned to Jess. With her hand clamped over her mouth, her shoulders shook with laughter.

"Jess, if you'll stop laughing for a minute. . ." Tom summoned his most serious tone. "Do you want to stay in New York or go to—"

"Go, go!" their friends shouted in unison.

Jess slipped her arm around his waist. "Wherever you go, I'll go."

A collective groan came from the peanut gallery. Tom waved them away. "Break it up, will you? The show is over."

A Letter To Our Readers

Dear Reader:

In order that we might better contribute to your reading enjoyment, we would appreciate your taking a few minutes to respond to the following questions. We welcome your comments and read each form and letter we receive. When completed, please return to the following:

Fiction Editor
Heartsong Presents
PO Box 719
Uhrichsville, Ohio 44683

1. Did you enjoy reading *Love Online* by Kristen Billerbeck and Nancy Toback?
   ❑ Very much! I would like to see more books by this author!
   ❑ Moderately. I would have enjoyed it more if

   _____

   _____

   _____

2. Are you a member of **Heartsong Presents**? ❑ Yes ❑ No
   If no, where did you purchase this book? _____

   _____

3. How would you rate, on a scale from 1 (poor) to 5 (superior), the cover design? _____

4. On a scale from 1 (poor) to 10 (superior), please rate the following elements.

   ____ Heroine   ____ Plot
   ____ Hero   ____ Inspirational theme
   ____ Setting   ____ Secondary characters

5. These characters were special because?_____

_____

_____

6. How has this book inspired your life?_____

_____

_____

7. What settings would you like to see covered in future
   Heartsong Presents books? _____

_____

_____

8. What are some inspirational themes you would like to see
   treated in future books? _____

_____

_____

9. Would you be interested in reading other **Heartsong
   Presents** titles? ❑ Yes ❑ No

10. Please check your age range:
    ❑ Under 18   ❑ 18-24
    ❑ 25-34   ❑ 35-45
    ❑ 46-55   ❑ Over 55

Name_____

Occupation _____

Address _____

City_____ State_____ Zip_____

Kaleidoscope

4 stories in 1

Perspective changes in Four suspense-filled romances by Lauralee Bliss, Gloria Brandt, DiAnn Mills, and Kathleen Paul.

Contemporary novels of mystery, suspense, love, and faith follow the lives of four women who wonder just how much of their hearts they can share with their romantic interests.

Contemporary, paperback, 480 pages, 5 ³/₁₆"x 8"

❤ ❤ ❤ ❤ ❤ ❤ ❤ ❤ ❤ ❤ ❤ ❤ ❤ ❤ ❤ ❤ ❤

❤ ❤ ❤ ❤ ❤ ❤ ❤ ❤ ❤ ❤ ❤ ❤ ❤ ❤ ❤ ❤ ❤

Presents

Great Inspirational Romance at a Great Price!